Dover Thrift Study Edition

Romeo and Juliet

WILLIAM SHAKESPEARE

DOVER PUBLICATIONS, INC.
Mineola, New York

Copyright

Copyright © 2009 by Dover Publications, Inc.
Pages 93–162 copyright © 1999, 1995 by Research & Education Association, Inc.
All rights reserved.

Bibliographical Note

This Dover edition, first published in 2009, contains the unabridged text of *Romeo and Juliet,* as published in Volume VI of the second edition of *The Works of William Shakespeare,* Macmillan and Co., London, 1892, plus literary analysis and perspectives from *MAXnotes® for Romeo and Juliet,* published in 1999 by Research & Education Association, Inc., Piscataway, New Jersey. The explanatory footnotes to the play were prepared specially for the present edition.

Library of Congress Cataloging-in-Publication Data

Shakespeare, William, 1564–1616.
    Romeo and Juliet / William Shakespeare.
       p. cm. — (Dover thrift study edition)
    ISBN-13: 978-0-486-47573-8 (alk. paper)
    ISBN-10: 0-486-47573-5 (alk. paper)
     1. Romeo (Fictitious character)—Drama. 2. Juliet (Fictitious character)—Drama. 3. Conflict of generations—Drama. 4. Vendetta—Drama. 5. Verona (Italy)—Drama. 6. Shakespeare, William, 1564–1616. Romeo and Juliet. I. Title.

PR2831.A2D63 2009
822.3'3—dc22

                                   2009026173

Manufactured in the United States by LSC Communications
47573505   2017
www.doverpublications.com

Publisher's Note

Combining the complete text of a classic novel or drama with a comprehensive study guide, Dover Thrift Study Editions are the most effective way to gain a thorough understanding of the major works of world literature.

The study guide features up-to-date and expert analysis of every chapter or section from the source work. Questions and fully explained answers follow, allowing readers to analyze the material critically. Character lists, author bios, and discussions of the work's historical context are also provided.

Each Dover Thrift Study Edition includes everything a student needs to prepare for homework, discussions, reports, and exams.

Contents

Romeo and Juliet

WILLIAM SHAKESPEARE

Contents

Dramatis Personae

ESCALUS, Prince of Verona.
PARIS, a young nobleman, kinsman to the Prince.
MONTAGUE,
CAPULET,   heads of two houses at variance with each other.
An old man, of the Capulet family.
ROMEO, son to Montague.
MERCUTIO, kinsman to the Prince, and friend to Romeo.
BENVOLIO, nephew to Montague, and friend to Romeo.
TYBALT, nephew to Lady Capulet.
FRIAR LAURENCE, a Franciscan.
FRIAR JOHN, of the same order.
BALTHASAR, servant to Romeo.
SAMPSON,
GREGORY,   servants to Capulet.
PETER, servant to Juliet's nurse.
ABRAHAM, servant to Montague.
An Apothecary.
Three Musicians.
Page to Paris; another Page; an Officer.

LADY MONTAGUE, wife to Montague.
LADY CAPULET, wife to Capulet.
JULIET, daughter to Capulet.
Nurse to Juliet.

Citizens of Verona; kinsfolk of both houses; Maskers, Guards, Watchmen, and Attendants.

Chorus.

SCENE: *Verona; Mantua.*

PROLOGUE.

Enter Chorus.

CHOR.   Two households, both alike in dignity,
    In fair Verona, where we lay our scene,
From ancient grudge break to new mutiny,
    Where civil blood makes civil hands unclean.
From forth the fatal loins of these two foes
    A pair of star-cross'd lovers take their life;
Whose misadventured piteous overthrows
    Do with their death bury their parents' strife.
The fearful passage of their death-mark'd love,
    And the continuance of their parents' rage,
Which, but their children's end, nought could remove,
    Is now the two hours' traffic of our stage;
The which if you with patient ears attend,
What here shall miss, our toil shall strive to mend.

ACT I.

Scene I. *Verona. A public place.*

Enter Sampson *and* Gregory, *of the house of Capulet, with swords and bucklers.*

SAM.   Gregory, on my word, we'll not carry coals.[1]

GRE.   No, for then we should be colliers.

SAM.   I mean, an we be in choler, we'll draw.

GRE.   Ay, while you live, draw your neck out o' the collar.[2]

SAM.   I strike quickly, being moved.

GRE.   But thou art not quickly moved to strike.

SAM.   A dog of the house of Montague moves me.

GRE.   To move is to stir, and to be valiant is to stand: therefore, if thou art moved, thou runn'st away.

SAM.   A dog of that house shall move me to stand: I will take the wall[3] of any man or maid of Montague's.

GRE.   That shows thee a weak slave; for the weakest goes to the wall.

SAM.   'Tis true; and therefore women, being the weaker vessels, are ever thrust to the wall: therefore I will push Montague's men from the wall and thrust his maids to the wall.

GRE.   The quarrel is between our masters and us their men.

SAM.   'Tis all one, I will show myself a tyrant: when I have fought with the men, I will be civil with the maids; I will cut off their heads.

GRE.   The heads of the maids?

SAM.   Ay, the heads of the maids, or their maidenheads; take it in what sense thou wilt.

GRE.   They must take it in sense that feel it.

---

[1] *carry coals*] tolerate insults.

[2] *collar*] hangman's noose.

[3] *take the wall*] walk on the side of the street nearest the wall; thus, insult.

SAM.   Me they shall feel while I am able to stand: and 'tis known I am a
       pretty piece of flesh.
GRE.   'Tis well thou art not fish; if thou hadst, thou hadst been poor
       John.⁴ Draw thy tool; here comes two of the house of Montagues.

Enter ABRAHAM *and* BALTHASAR.

SAM.   My naked weapon is out: quarrel; I will back thee.
GRE.   How! turn thy back and run?
SAM.   Fear me not.
GRE.   No, marry: I fear thee!
SAM.   Let us take the law of our sides; let them begin.
GRE.   I will frown as I pass by, and let them take it as they list.
SAM.   Nay, as they dare. I will bite my thumb at them; which is a
       disgrace to them, if they bear it.
ABR.   Do you bite your thumb at us, sir?
SAM.   I do bite my thumb, sir.
ABR.   Do you bite your thumb at us, sir?
SAM.   [*Aside to* GRE.] Is the law of our side, if I say ay?
GRE.   No.
SAM.   No, sir, I do not bite my thumb at you, sir; but I bite my thumb,
       sir.
GRE.   Do you quarrel, sir?
ABR.   Quarrel, sir! no, sir.
SAM.   But if you do, sir, I am for you: I serve as good a man as you.
ABR.   No better.
SAM.   Well, sir.

Enter BENVOLIO.

GRE.   [*Aside to* SAM.] Say 'better': here comes one of my master's
       kinsmen.
SAM.   Yes, better, sir.
ABR.   You lie.
SAM.   Draw, if you be men. Gregory, remember thy swashing⁵ blow.
                                                        [*They fight.*
BEN.   Part, fools!   [*Beating down their weapons.*
       Put up your swords; you know not what you do.

---

⁴ *poor John*] salted and dried hake, a coarse kind of fish.
⁵ *swashing*] smashing.

Enter TYBALT.

TYB.   What, art thou drawn among these heartless hinds?[6]
        Turn thee, Benvolio, look upon thy death.
BEN.   I do but keep the peace: put up thy sword,
        Or manage it to part these men with me.
TYB.   What, drawn, and talk of peace! I hate the word,
        As I hate hell, all Montagues, and thee:
        Have at thee, coward!   [*They fight.*

Enter several of both houses, who join the fray; then enter Citizens *and* Peace-officers, *with clubs.*

FIRST OFF.   Clubs, bills,[7] and partisans! strike! beat them down!
        Down with the Capulets! down with the Montagues!

Enter old CAPULET *in his gown, and* LADY CAPULET.

CAP.   What noise is this? Give me my long sword, ho!
LA. CAP.   A crutch, a crutch! why call you for a sword?
CAP.   My sword, I say! Old Montague is come,
        And flourishes his blade in spite of me.

Enter old MONTAGUE *and* LADY MONTAGUE.

MON.   Thou villain Capulet!—Hold me not, let me go.
LA. MON.   Thou shalt not stir one foot to seek a foe.

Enter PRINCE ESCALUS, *with his train.*

PRIN.   Rebellious subjects, enemies to peace,
        Profaners of this neighbour-stained steel,—
        Will they not hear? What, ho! you men, you beasts,
        That quench the fire of your pernicious rage
        With purple fountains issuing from your veins,
        On pain of torture, from those bloody hands
        Throw your mistemper'd weapons to the ground,
        And hear the sentence of your moved prince.
        Three civil brawls, bred of an airy word,
        By thee, old Capulet, and Montague,
        Have thrice disturb'd the quiet of our streets,
        And made Verona's ancient citizens

---

[6] *heartless hinds*] (1) cowardly menials; (2) female deer unprotected by a hart.
[7] *bills*] a kind of pike or halberd.

Cast by their grave beseeming ornaments,
To wield old partisans, in hands as old,
Canker'd with peace, to part your canker'd hate:
If ever you disturb our streets again,
Your lives shall pay the forfeit of the peace.
For this time, all the rest depart away:
You, Capulet, shall go along with me;
And, Montague, come you this afternoon,
To know our farther pleasure in this case,
To old Free-town, our common judgement-place.
Once more, on pain of death, all men depart.

[*Exeunt all but* MONTAGUE, LADY MONTAGUE, *and* BENVOLIO.

MON.   Who set this ancient quarrel new abroach?
         Speak, nephew, were you by when it began?
BEN.   Here were the servants of your adversary
         And yours close fighting ere I did approach:
         I drew to part them: in the instant came
         The fiery Tybalt, with his sword prepared;
         Which, as he breathed defiance to my ears,
         He swung about his head, and cut the winds,
         Who, nothing hurt withal, hiss'd him in scorn:
         While we were interchanging thrusts and blows,
         Came more and more, and fought on part and part,[8]
         Till the Prince came, who parted either part.
LA. MON.   O, where is Romeo? saw you him to-day?
         Right glad I am he was not at this fray.
BEN.   Madam, an hour before the worshipp'd sun
         Peer'd forth the golden window of the east,
         A troubled mind drave me to walk abroad;
         Where, underneath the grove of sycamore
         That westward rooteth from the city's side,
         So early walking did I see your son:
         Towards him I made; but he was ware of me,
         And stole into the covert of the wood:
         I, measuring his affections[9] by my own,
         Which then most sought where most might not be found,
         Being one too many by my weary self,

---

[8] *on part and part*] on one side and the other.
[9] *affections*] wishes, inclination.

Pursued my humour, not pursuing his,
And gladly shunn'd who gladly fled from me.
MON.   Many a morning hath he there been seen,
With tears augmenting the fresh morning's dew,
Adding to clouds more clouds with his deep sighs:
But all so soon as the all-cheering sun
Should in the farthest east begin to draw
The shady curtains from Aurora's bed,
Away from light steals home my heavy son,
And private in his chamber pens himself,
Shuts up his windows, locks fair daylight out,
And makes himself an artificial night:
Black and portentous must this humour prove,
Unless good counsel may the cause remove.
BEN.   My noble uncle, do you know the cause?
MON.   I neither know it nor can learn of him.
BEN.   Have you importuned him by any means?
MON.   Both by myself and many other friends:
But he, his own affections' counsellor,
Is to himself—I will not say how true—
But to himself so secret and so close,
So far from sounding and discovery,
As is the bud bit with an envious worm,
Ere he can spread his sweet leaves to the air,
Or dedicate his beauty to the sun.
Could we but learn from whence his sorrows grow,
We would as willingly give cure as know.

Enter ROMEO.

BEN.   See, where he comes: so please you step aside;
I'll know his grievance, or be much denied.
MON.   I would thou wert so happy by thy stay,
To hear true shrift. Come, madam, let's away.
                                    [*Exeunt* MONTAGUE *and* LADY.
BEN.   Good morrow, cousin.
ROM.   Is the day so young?
BEN.   But new struck nine.
ROM.   Ay me! sad hours seem long.
   Was that my father that went hence so fast?
BEN.   It was. What sadness lengthens Romeo's hours?
ROM.   Not having that which, having, makes them short.
BEN.   In love?

ROM.   Out—
BEN.   Of love?
ROM.   Out of her favour, where I am in love.
BEN.   Alas, that love, so gentle in his view,
        Should be so tyrannous and rough in proof![10]
ROM.   Alas, that love, whose view is muffled still,
        Should without eyes see pathways to his will!
        Where shall we dine? O me! What fray was here?
        Yet tell me not, for I have heard it all.
        Here's much to do with hate, but more with love:
        Why, then, O brawling love! O loving hate!
        O any thing, of nothing first create!
        O heavy lightness! serious vanity!
        Mis-shapen chaos of well-seeming forms!
        Feather of lead, bright smoke, cold fire, sick health!
        Still-waking sleep, that is not what it is!
        This love feel I, that feel no love in this.
        Dost thou not laugh?
BEN.   No, coz, I rather weep.
ROM.   Good heart, at what?
BEN.   At thy good heart's oppression.
ROM.   Why, such is love's transgression.
        Griefs of mine own lie heavy in my breast;
        Which thou wilt propagate,[11] to have it prest
        With more of thine: this love that thou hast shown
        Doth add more grief to too much of mine own.
        Love is a smoke raised with the fume of sighs;
        Being purged, a fire sparkling in lovers' eyes;
        Being vex'd, a sea nourish'd with lovers' tears:
        What is it else? a madness most discreet,
        A choking gall and a preserving sweet.
        Farewell, my coz.
BEN.   Soft! I will go along:
        An if you leave me so, you do me wrong.
ROM.   Tut, I have lost myself; I am not here;
        This is not Romeo, he's some other where.
BEN.   Tell me in sadness,[12] who is that you love?
ROM.   What, shall I groan and tell thee?

[10] *proof*] experience.
[11] *propagate*] increase.
[12] *sadness*] seriousness.

BEN.   Groan! why, no;
  But sadly tell me who.
ROM.   Bid a sick man in sadness make his will:
    Ah, word ill urged to one that is so ill!
    In sadness, cousin, I do love a woman.
BEN.   I aim'd so near when I supposed you loved.
ROM.   A right good mark-man! And she's fair I love.
BEN.   A right fair mark, fair coz, is soonest hit.
ROM.   Well, in that hit you miss: she'll not be hit
    With Cupid's arrow; she hath Dian's wit,
    And in strong proof[13] of chastity well arm'd,
    From love's weak childish bow she lives unharm'd.
    She will not stay[14] the siege of loving terms,
    Nor bide the encounter of assailing eyes,
    Nor ope her lap to saint-seducing gold:
    O, she is rich in beauty, only poor
    That, when she dies, with beauty dies her store.
BEN.   Then she hath sworn that she will still[15] live chaste?
ROM.   She hath, and in that sparing makes huge waste;
    For beauty, starved with her severity,
    Cuts beauty off from all posterity.
    She is too fair, too wise, wisely too fair,
    To merit bliss by making me despair:
    She hath forsworn to love; and in that vow
    Do I live dead, that live to tell it now.
BEN.   Be ruled by me, forget to think of her.
ROM.   O, teach me how I should forget to think.
BEN.   By giving liberty unto thine eyes;
    Examine other beauties.
ROM.   'Tis the way
    To call hers, exquisite, in question more:[16]
    These happy masks that kiss fair ladies' brows,
    Being black, put us in mind they hide the fair;
    He that is strucken blind cannot forget
    The precious treasure of his eyesight lost:
    Show me a mistress that is passing[17] fair,

---

[13] *proof*] impenetrable armor.
[14] *stay*] undergo, endure.
[15] *still*] always.
[16] *in question more*] even more strongly to mind.
[17] *passing*] exceedingly.

       What doth her beauty serve but as a note
       Where I may read who pass'd that passing fair?
       Farewell: thou canst not teach me to forget.
BEN.   I'll pay that doctrine,[18] or else die in debt.   [*Exeunt.*

SCENE II. *A street.*

Enter CAPULET, PARIS, *and* Servant.

CAP.   But Montague is bound as well as I,
       In penalty alike; and 'tis not hard, I think,
       For men so old as we to keep the peace.
PAR.   Of honourable reckoning[1] are you both;
       And pity 'tis you lived at odds so long.
       But now, my lord, what say you to my suit?
CAP.   But saying o'er what I have said before:
       My child is yet a stranger in the world;
       She hath not seen the change of fourteen years:
       Let two more summers wither in their pride
       Ere we may think her ripe to be a bride.
PAR.   Younger than she are happy mothers made.
CAP.   And too soon marr'd are those so early made.
       The earth hath swallow'd all my hopes but she,
       She is the hopeful lady of my earth:[2]
       But woo her, gentle Paris, get her heart;
       My will to her consent is but a part;
       An she agree, within her scope of choice
       Lies my consent and fair according voice.
       This night I hold an old accustom'd feast,
       Whereto I have invited many a guest,
       Such as I love; and you among the store,
       One more, most welcome, makes my number more.
       At my poor house look to behold this night
       Earth-treading stars that make dark heaven light:
       Such comfort as do lusty young men feel
       When well-apparell'd April on the heel

[18] *pay that doctrine*] give that instruction.

---

[1] *reckoning*] repute.
[2] *hopeful . . . earth*] heir of my property and line.

Of limping winter treads, even such delight
Among fresh female buds shall you this night
Inherit at my house; hear all, all see,
And like her most whose merit most shall be:
Which on more view, of many mine being one
May stand in number, though in reckoning none.
Come, go with me. [*To Servant*] Go, sirrah, trudge about
Through fair Verona; find those persons out
Whose names are written there, and to them say,
My house and welcome on their pleasure stay.

[*Exeunt* CAPULET *and* PARIS.

SERV.   Find them out whose names are written here! It is written that the
shoemaker should meddle with his yard and the tailor with his last, [3]
the fisher with his pencil and the painter with his nets; but I am sent
to find those persons whose names are here writ, and can never find
what names the writing person hath here writ. I must to the learned.
In good time.

Enter BENVOLIO *and* ROMEO.

BEN.   Tut, man, one fire burns out another's burning.
           One pain is lessen'd by another's anguish;
        Turn giddy, and be holp by backward turning;
           One desperate grief cures with another's languish:
        Take thou some new infection to thy eye,
        And the rank poison of the old will die.

ROM.   Your plantain-leaf is excellent for that.

BEN.   For what, I pray thee?

ROM.   For your broken shin.

BEN.   Why, Romeo, art thou mad?

ROM.   Not mad, but bound more than a madman is;
        Shut up in prison, kept without my food,
        Whipt and tormented and— God-den, [4] good fellow.

SERV.   God gi' god-den. I pray, sir, can you read?

ROM.   Ay, mine own fortune in my misery.

SERV.   Perhaps you have learned it without book: but, I pray, can you
read any thing you see?

ROM.   Ay, if I know the letters and the language.

SERV.   Ye say honestly: rest you merry!

ROM.   Stay, fellow; I can read.   [*Reads.*

---

[3] *last*] the mold on which shoes are made.
[4] *God-den*] Good evening.

'Signior Martino and his wife and daughters; County Anselme and his beauteous sisters; the lady widow of Vitruvio; Signior Placentio and his lovely nieces; Mercutio and his brother Valentine; mine uncle Capulet, his wife, and daughters; my fair niece Rosaline; Livia; Signior Valentio and his cousin Tybalt; Lucio and the lively Helena.'

A fair assembly: whither should they come?

SERV.   Up.[5]

ROM.   Whither? to supper?

SERV.   To our house.

ROM.   Whose house?

SERV.   My master's.

ROM.   Indeed, I should have ask'd you that before.

SERV.   Now I'll tell you without asking: my master is the great rich Capulet; and if you be not of the house of Montagues, I pray, come and crush a cup of wine. Rest you merry!   [*Exit.*

BEN.   At this same ancient feast of Capulet's
        Sups the fair Rosaline whom thou so lovest,
        With all the admired beauties of Verona:
        Go thither, and with unattainted[6] eye
        Compare her face with some that I shall show,
        And I will make thee think thy swan a crow.

ROM.   When the devout religion of mine eye
            Maintains such falsehood, then turn tears to fires;
        And these, who, often drown'd, could never die,
            Transparent heretics, be burnt for liars!
        One fairer than my love! the all-seeing sun
        Ne'er saw her match since first the world begun.

BEN.   Tut, you saw her fair, none else being by,
        Herself poised with herself in either eye:
        But in that crystal scales let there be weigh'd
        Your lady's love against some other maid,
        That I will show you shining at this feast,
        And she shall scant show well that now seems best.

ROM.   I'll go along, no such sight to be shown,
        But to rejoice in splendour of mine own.   [*Exeunt.*

---

[5] *come . . . Up*] The servant is quibbling, "come up" being a vulgar phrase.

[6] *unattainted*] not infected, impartial.

SCENE III. *A room in Capulet's house.*

Enter LADY CAPULET *and* NURSE.

LA. CAP. Nurse, where's my daughter? call her forth to me.
NURSE. Now, by my maidenhead at twelve year old,
 I bade her come. What, lamb! what, lady-bird!
 God forbid!—Where's this girl? What, Juliet!

Enter JULIET.

JUL. How now! who calls?
NURSE. Your mother.
JUL. Madam, I am here. What is your will?
LA. CAP. This is the matter. Nurse, give leave awhile,
 We must talk in secret:—Nurse, come back again;
 I have remember'd me, thou's¹ hear our counsel.
 Thou know'st my daughter's of a pretty age.
NURSE. Faith, I can tell her age unto an hour.
LA. CAP. She's not fourteen.
NURSE.   I'll lay fourteen of my teeth,—
 And yet, to my teen² be it spoken, I have but four,—
 She is not fourteen. How long is it now
 To Lammas-tide?
LA. CAP. A fortnight and odd days.
NURSE. Even or odd, of all days in the year,
 Come Lammas-eve at night shall she be fourteen.
 Susan and she—God rest all Christian souls!—
 Were of an age: well, Susan is with God;
 She was too good for me:—but, as I said,
 On Lammas-eve at night shall she be fourteen;
 That shall she, marry; I remember it well.
 'Tis since the earthquake now eleven years;
 And she was wean'd,—I never shall forget it—
 Of all the days of the year, upon that day:
 For I had then laid wormwood³ to my dug,
 Sitting in the sun under the dove-house wall;

¹ *thou's*] thou shalt.
² *teen*] grief, pain.
³ *wormwood*] *Artemisia absinthium*, proverbial for its bitterness and medicinal proper-
 ties.

My lord and you were then at Mantua:—
Nay, I do bear a brain:—but, as I said,
When it did taste the wormwood on the nipple
Of my dug, and felt it bitter, pretty fool,
To see it tetchy, and fall out with the dug!
Shake, quoth the dove-house: 'twas no need, I trow,
To bid me trudge.
And since that time it is eleven years;
For then she could stand high-lone;[4] nay, by the rood,
She could have run and waddled all about;
For even the day before, she broke her brow:[5]
And then my husband,—God be with his soul!
A' was a merry man—took up the child:
'Yea,' quoth he, 'dost thou fall upon thy face?
Thou wilt fall backward when thou hast more wit;
Wilt thou not, Jule?' and, by my holidame,[6]
The pretty wretch left crying, and said 'Ay.'
To see now how a jest shall come about!
I warrant, an I should live a thousand years,
I never should forget it: 'Wilt thou not, Jule?' quoth he;
And, pretty fool, it stinted,[7] and said 'Ay.'

LA. CAP.   Enough of this; I pray thee, hold thy peace.

NURSE.   Yes, madam: yet I cannot choose but laugh,
To think it should leave crying, and say 'Ay':
And yet, I warrant, it had upon it brow
A bump as big as a young cockerel's stone;[8]
A perilous knock; and it cried bitterly:
'Yea,' quoth my husband, 'fall'st upon thy face?
Thou wilt fall backward when thou comest to age;
Wilt thou not, Jule?' It stinted, and said 'Ay.'

JUL.   And stint thou too, I pray thee, Nurse, say I.

NURSE.   Peace, I have done. God mark thee to his grace!
Thou wast the prettiest babe that e'er I nursed:
An I might live to see thee married once,[9]
I have my wish.

LA. CAP.   Marry, that 'marry' is the very theme

---

[4] *high-lone*] on her own feet, unsupported.
[5] *broke her brow*] (fell and) cut her head.
[6] *holidame*] halidom, salvation.
[7] *stinted*] ceased.
[8] *stone*] testicle.
[9] *once*] ever, at some time.

     I came to talk of. Tell me, daughter Juliet,
     How stands your disposition to be married?

Jul.   It is an honour that I dream not of.

Nurse.   An honour! were not I thine only nurse,
     I would say thou hadst suck'd wisdom from thy teat.

La. Cap.   Well, think of marriage now; younger than you
     Here in Verona, ladies of esteem,
     Are made already mothers. By my count,
     I was your mother much upon these years
     That you are now a maid. Thus then in brief;
     The valiant Paris seeks you for his love.

Nurse.   A man, young lady! lady, such a man
     As all the world—why, he's a man of wax. [10]

La. Cap.   Verona's summer hath not such a flower.

Nurse.   Nay, he's a flower; in faith, a very flower.

La. Cap.   What say you? can you love the gentleman?
     This night you shall behold him at our feast:
     Read o'er the volume of young Paris' face,
     And find delight writ there with beauty's pen;
     Examine every married [11] lineament,
     And see how one another lends content;
     And what obscured in this fair volume lies
     Find written in the margent of his eyes.
     This precious book of love, this unbound lover,
     To beautify him, only lacks a cover:
     The fish lives in the sea; and 'tis much pride
     For fair without the fair within to hide:
     That book in many's eyes doth share the glory,
     That in gold clasps locks in the golden story:
     So shall you share all that he doth possess,
     By having him making yourself no less.

Nurse.   No less! nay, bigger: women grow by men.

La. Cap.   Speak briefly, can you like of Paris' love?

Jul.   I'll look to like, if looking liking move:
     But no more deep will I endart mine eye
     Than your consent gives strength to make it fly.

Enter a Servingman.

---

[10] *a man of wax*] as handsome as if modeled in wax.
[11] *married*] proportioned.

SERV.   Madam, the guests are come, supper served up, you called, my
    young lady asked for, the Nurse cursed in the pantry, and every
    thing in extremity. I must hence to wait; I beseech you, follow
    straight.
LA. CAP.   We follow thee. [*Exit* Servingman.] Juliet, the County stays.
NURSE.   Go, girl, seek happy nights to happy days.   [*Exeunt.*

SCENE IV. *A street.*

Enter ROMEO, MERCUTIO, BENVOLIO, *with five or six other* Maskers, *and*
Torch-bearers.

ROM.   What, shall this speech be spoke for our excuse?
    Or shall we on without apology?
BEN.   The date is out of such prolixity:
    We'll have no Cupid hoodwink'd[1] with a scarf,
    Bearing a Tartar's painted bow of lath,
    Scaring the ladies like a crow-keeper;[2]
    Nor no without-book prologue, faintly spoke
    After the prompter, for our entrance:
    But, let them measure us by what they will,
    We'll measure them a measure,[3] and be gone.
ROM.   Give me a torch: I am not for this ambling;[4]
    Being but heavy, I will bear the light.
MER.   Nay, gentle Romeo, we must have you dance.
ROM.   Not I, believe me: you have dancing shoes
    With nimble soles: I have a soul of lead
    So stakes me to the ground, I cannot move.
MER.   You are a lover; borrow Cupid's wings,
    And soar with them above a common bound.
ROM.   I am too sore enpierced with his shaft
    To soar with his light feathers, and so bound,
    I cannot bound a pitch[5] above dull woe:
    Under love's heavy burthen do I sink.

---

[1] *hoodwink'd*] blindfolded.
[2] *crow-keeper*] scarecrow.
[3] *measure them a measure*] dance.
[4] *ambling*] affected movement, as in a dance.
[5] *pitch*] height to which the falcon soars before swooping down for the kill.

MER.   And, to sink in it, should you burthen love;
   Too great oppression for a tender thing.

ROM.   Is love a tender thing? it is too rough,
   Too rude, too boisterous, and it pricks like thorn.

MER.   If love be rough with you, be rough with love;
   Prick love for pricking, and you beat love down.
   Give me a case[6] to put my visage in:
   A visor for a visor! what care I
   What curious eye doth quote[7] deformities?
   Here are the beetle-brows shall blush for me.

BEN.   Come, knock and enter, and no sooner in
   But every man betake him to his legs.

ROM.   A torch for me: let wantons light of heart
   Tickle the senseless rushes with their heels;
   For I am proverb'd with a grandsire phrase;
   I'll be a candle-holder, and look on.
   The game was ne'er so fair, and I am done.

MER.   Tut, dun's the mouse,[8] the constable's own word:
   If thou art dun, we'll draw thee from the mire
   Of this sir-reverence[9] love, wherein thou stick'st
   Up to the ears. Come, we burn daylight, ho.

ROM.   Nay, that's not so.

MER.   I mean, sir, in delay
   We waste our lights in vain, like lamps by day.
   Take our good[10] meaning, for our judgement sits
   Five times in that ere once in our five wits.

ROM.   And we mean well, in going to this mask;
   But 'tis no wit to go.

MER.   Why, may one ask?

ROM.   I dreamt a dream to-night.

MER.   And so did I.

ROM.   Well, what was yours?

MER.   That dreamers often lie.

ROM.   In bed asleep, while they do dream things true.

MER.   O, then, I see Queen Mab hath been with you.
   She is the fairies' midwife, and she comes
   In shape no bigger than an agate-stone

---

   [6] *case*] mask.
   [7] *quote*] perceive.
   [8] *dun's the mouse*] a proverbial expression meaning "stay still."
   [9] *sir-reverence*] a corruption of "save your reverence," a form of apology.
   [10] *good*] intended.

On the fore-finger of an alderman,
Drawn with a team of little atomies[11]
Athwart men's noses as they lie asleep:
Her waggon-spokes made of long spinners' legs;
The cover, of the wings of grasshoppers;
Her traces, of the smallest spider's web;
Her collars, of the moonshine's watery beams;
Her whip, of cricket's bone; the lash, of film;[12]
Her waggoner, a small grey-coated gnat,
Not half so big as a round little worm
Prick'd from the lazy finger of a maid:
Her chariot is an empty hazel-nut,
Made by the joiner squirrel or old grub,
Time out o' mind the fairies' coachmakers.
And in this state she gallops night by night
Through lovers' brains, and then they dream of love;
O'er courtiers' knees, that dream on court'sies straight;[13]
O'er lawyers' fingers, who straight dream on fees;
O'er ladies' lips, who straight on kisses dream,
Which oft the angry Mab with blisters plagues,
Because their breaths with sweetmeats tainted are:
Sometime she gallops o'er a courtier's nose,
And then dreams he of smelling out a suit;
And sometime comes she with a tithe-pig's tail
Tickling a parson's nose as a' lies asleep,
Then dreams he of another benefice:
Sometime she driveth o'er a soldier's neck,
And then dreams he of cutting foreign throats,
Of breaches, ambuscadoes, Spanish blades,
Of healths five fathom deep; and then anon
Drums in his ear, at which he starts and wakes,
And being thus frighted swears a prayer or two,
And sleeps again. This is that very Mab
That plats the manes of horses in the night,
And bakes the elf-locks[14] in foul sluttish hairs,
Which once untangled much misfortune bodes:
This is the hag, when maids lie on their backs,
That presses them and learns them first to bear,

[11] *atomies*] tiny creatures.
[12] *film*] gossamer.
[13] *straight*] immediately.
[14] *elf-locks*] tangles.

Making them women of good carriage:
This is she—

ROM.   Peace, peace, Mercutio, peace!
Thou talk'st of nothing.

MER.   True, I talk of dreams;
Which are the children of an idle brain,
Begot of nothing but vain fantasy,
Which is as thin of substance as the air,
And more inconstant than the wind, who wooes
Even now the frozen bosom of the north,
And, being anger'd, puffs away from thence,
Turning his face to the dew-dropping south.

BEN.   This wind you talk of blows us from ourselves;
Supper is done, and we shall come too late.

ROM.   I fear, too early: for my mind misgives
Some consequence, yet hanging in the stars,
Shall bitterly begin his fearful date[15]
With this night's revels, and expire the term
Of a despised life closed in my breast,
By some vile forfeit of untimely death:
But He, that hath the steerage of my course,
Direct my sail! On, lusty gentlemen.

BEN.   Strike, drum.   [*Exeunt.*

SCENE V. *A hall in Capulet's house.*

Musicians *waiting.* Enter Servingmen, *with napkins.*

FIRST SERV.   Where's Potpan, that he helps not to take away? he shift a
trencher![1] he scrape a trencher!

SEC. SERV.   When good manners shall lie all in one or two men's hands,
and they unwashed too, 'tis a foul thing.

FIRST SERV.   Away with the joint-stools,[2] remove the court-cupboard,[3]
look to the plate. Good thou, save me a piece of marchpane;[4] and,
as thou lovest me, let the porter let in Susan Grindstone and Nell.
Antony, and Potpan!

[15] *date*] time, duration.

---

[1] *trencher*] plate.
[2] *joint-stools*] wooden stools.
[3] *court-cupboard*] movable buffet or closet.
[4] *marchpane*] sweet biscuit made of sugar and almonds.

SEC. SERV.   Ay, boy, ready.

FIRST SERV.   You are looked for and called for, asked for and sought for,
     in the great chamber.

THIRD SERV.   We cannot be here and there too. Cheerly, boys; be brisk a
     while, and the longer liver take all.   [*They retire behind.*

Enter CAPULET, *with* JULIET *and others of his house, meeting the* Guests
and Maskers.

CAP.   Welcome, gentlemen! ladies that have their toes
     Unplagued with corns will have a bout with you:
     Ah ha, my mistresses! which of you all
     Will now deny to dance? she that makes dainty,
     She, I'll swear, hath corns; am I come near ye now?
     Welcome, gentlemen! I have seen the day
     That I have worn a visor, and could tell
     A whispering tale in a fair lady's ear,
     Such as would please: 'tis gone, 'tis gone, 'tis gone:
     You are welcome, gentlemen! Come, musicians, play.
     A hall, a hall! give room! and foot it, girls.
                      [*Music plays, and they dance.*
     More light, you knaves; and turn the tables up,
     And quench the fire, the room is grown too hot.
     Ah, sirrah, this unlook'd-for sport comes well.
     Nay, sit, nay, sit, good cousin Capulet;
     For you and I are past our dancing days:
     How long is't now since last yourself and I
     Were in a mask?

SEC. CAP.   By'r lady, thirty years.

CAP.   What, man! 'tis not so much, 'tis not so much:
     'Tis since the nuptial of Lucentio,
     Come Pentecost as quickly as it will,
     Some five and twenty years; and then we mask'd.

SEC. CAP.   'Tis more, 'tis more: his son is elder, sir;
     His son is thirty.

CAP.   Will you tell me that?
     His son was but a ward two years ago.

ROM.   [*To a* Servingman] What lady's that, which doth enrich the hand
     Of yonder knight?

SERV.   I know not, sir.

ROM.   O, she doth teach the torches to burn bright!
     It seems she hangs upon the cheek of night

    Like a rich jewel in an Ethiop's ear;
    Beauty too rich for use, for earth too dear!
    So shows a snowy dove trooping with crows,
    As yonder lady o'er her fellows shows.
    The measure done, I'll watch her place of stand,
    And, touching hers, make blessed my rude hand.
    Did my heart love till now? forswear it, sight!
    For I ne'er saw true beauty till this night.

TYB.   This, by his voice, should be a Montague.
    Fetch me my rapier, boy. What dares the slave
    Come hither, cover'd with an antic face,[5]
    To fleer[6] and scorn at our solemnity?
    Now, by the stock and honour of my kin,
    To strike him dead I hold it not a sin.

CAP.   Why, how now, kinsman! wherefore storm you so?

TYB.   Uncle, this is a Montague, our foe;
    A villain, that is hither come in spite,
    To scorn at our solemnity this night.

CAP.   Young Romeo is it?

TYB.   'Tis he, that villain Romeo.

CAP.   Content thee, gentle coz, let him alone,
    He bears him like a portly[7] gentleman;
    And, to say truth, Verona brags of him
    To be a virtuous and well-govern'd youth:
    I would not for the wealth of all this town
    Here in my house do him disparagement:
    Therefore be patient, take no note of him:
    It is my will, the which if thou respect,
    Show a fair presence and put off these frowns,
    An ill-beseeming semblance for a feast.

TYB.   It fits, when such a villain is a guest:
    I'll not endure him.

CAP.   He shall be endured:
    What, goodman[8] boy! I say, he shall: go to;
    Am I the master here, or you? go to.
    You'll not endure him! God shall mend my soul,

---

[5] *antic face*] odd-looking mask.
[6] *fleer*] grin mockingly.
[7] *portly*] well-bred, dignified.
[8] *goodman*] below the rank of gentleman.

         You'll make a mutiny among my guests!
         You will set cock-a-hoop![9] you'll be the man!
TYB.   Why, uncle, 'tis a shame.
CAP.   Go to, go to;
         You are a saucy boy: is't so, indeed?
         This trick may chance to scathe you, I know what:
         You must contrary me! marry, 'tis time.
         Well said, my hearts! You are a princox; go:
         Be quiet, or— More light, more light! For shame!
         I'll make you quiet. What, cheerly, my hearts!
TYB.   Patience perforce with wilful choler meeting
         Makes my flesh tremble in their different greeting.
         I will withdraw: but this intrusion shall,
         Now seeming sweet, convert to bitterest gall.   [*Exit.*
ROM.   [*To* JULIET] If I profane with my unworthiest hand
            This holy shrine, the gentle fine is this,
         My lips, two blushing pilgrims, ready stand
            To smooth that rough touch with a tender kiss.
JUL.   Good pilgrim, you do wrong your hand too much,
            Which mannerly devotion shows in this;
         For saints have hands that pilgrims' hands do touch,
            And palm to palm is holy palmers' kiss.
ROM.   Have not saints lips, and holy palmers too?
JUL.   Ay, pilgrim, lips that they must use in prayer.
ROM.   O, then, dear saint, let lips do what hands do;
            They pray, grant thou, lest faith turn to despair.
JUL.   Saints do not move, though grant for prayers' sake.
ROM.   Then move not, while my prayer's effect I take.
         Thus from my lips by thine my sin is purged.   [*Kissing her.*
JUL.   Then have my lips the sin that they have took.
ROM.   Sin from my lips? O trespass sweetly urged!
         Give me my sin again.
JUL.   You kiss by the book.
NURSE. Madam, your mother craves a word with you.
ROM.   What is her mother?
NURSE.   Marry, bachelor,
         Her mother is the lady of the house,
         And a good lady, and a wise and virtuous:
         I nursed her daughter, that you talk'd withal;

_____

[9] *set cock-a-hoop*] pick a quarrel.

I tell you, he that can lay hold of her
Shall have the chinks.[10]

ROM.   Is she a Capulet?
O dear account! my life is my foe's debt.

BEN.   Away, be gone; the sport is at the best.

ROM.   Ay, so I fear; the more is my unrest.

CAP.   Nay, gentlemen, prepare not to be gone;
We have a trifling foolish[11] banquet towards.[12]
Is it e'en so? why, then, I thank you all;
I thank you, honest gentlemen; good night.
More torches here! Come on then, let's to bed.
Ah, sirrah, by my fay, it waxes late:
I'll to my rest.   [*Exeunt all but* JULIET *and* NURSE.

JUL.   Come hither, Nurse. What is yond gentleman?

NURSE.   The son and heir of old Tiberio.

JUL.   What's he that now is going out of door?

NURSE.   Marry, that, I think, be young Petruchio.

JUL.   What's he that follows there, that would not dance?

NURSE.   I know not.

JUL.   Go ask his name. If he be married,
My grave is like to be my wedding bed.

NURSE.   His name is Romeo, and a Montague,
The only son of your great enemy.

JUL.   My only love sprung from my only hate!
Too early seen unknown, and known too late!
Prodigious birth of love it is to me,
That I must love a loathed enemy.

NURSE.   What's this? what's this?

JUL.   A rhyme I learn'd even now
Of one I danced withal.   [*One calls within 'Juliet.'*

NURSE.   Anon, anon!
Come, let's away; the strangers all are gone.   [*Exeunt.*

---

[10] *have the chinks*] acquire a financial fortune.
[11] *foolish*] small-scale.
[12] *towards*] in preparation.

ACT II.

PROLOGUE.

Enter Chorus.

CHOR.   Now old desire doth in his death-bed lie,
    And young affection gapes to be his heir;
That fair for which love groan'd for and would die,
    With tender Juliet match'd, is now not fair.
Now Romeo is beloved and loves again,
    Alike bewitched by the charm of looks,
But to his foe supposed he must complain,
    And she steal love's sweet bait from fearful hooks:
Being held a foe, he may not have access
    To breathe such vows as lovers use to swear;
And she as much in love, her means much less
    To meet her new beloved any where:
But passion lends them power, time means, to meet,
Tempering extremities with extreme sweet.   [*Exit.*

SCENE I. *A lane by the wall of Capulet's orchard.*

Enter ROMEO, *alone.*

ROM.   Can I go forward when my heart is here?
    Turn back, dull earth, and find thy centre out.
                [*He climbs the wall, and leaps down within it.*

Enter BENVOLIO *with* MERCUTIO.

BEN.   Romeo! my cousin Romeo!
MER.   He is wise;

    And, on my life, hath stol'n him home to bed.
BEN.   He ran this way, and leap'd this orchard wall:
    Call, good Mercutio.
MER.   Nay, I'll conjure too.
    Romeo! humours! madman! passion! lover!
    Appear thou in the likeness of a sigh:
    Speak but one rhyme, and I am satisfied;
    Cry but 'ay me!' pronounce but 'love' and 'dove';
    Speak to my gossip Venus one fair word,
    One nick-name for her purblind son and heir,
    Young Adam Cupid, he that shot so trim
    When King Cophetua[1] loved the beggar-maid!
    He heareth not, he stirreth not, he moveth not;
    The ape[2] is dead, and I must conjure him.
    I conjure thee by Rosaline's bright eyes,
    By her high forehead and her scarlet lip,
    By her fine foot, straight leg and quivering thigh,
    And the demesnes that there adjacent lie,
    That in thy likeness thou appear to us!
BEN.   An if he hear thee, thou wilt anger him.
MER.   This cannot anger him: 'twould anger him
    To raise a spirit in his mistress' circle
    Of some strange[3] nature, letting it there stand
    Till she had laid it and conjured it down;
    That were some spite: my invocation
    Is fair and honest, and in his mistress' name
    I conjure only but to raise up him.
BEN.   Come, he hath hid himself among these trees,
    To be consorted[4] with the humorous[5] night:
    Blind is his love, and best befits the dark.
MER.   If love be blind, love cannot hit the mark.
    Now will he sit under a medlar-tree,
    And wish his mistress were that kind of fruit
    As maids call medlars when they laugh alone.
    O, Romeo, that she were, O, that she were
    An open et cetera, thou a poperin pear![6]

---

[1] *King Cophetua*] a legendary figure who married a beggar.
[2] *ape*] a term of endearment.
[3] *strange*] other person's.
[4] *consorted*] associated.
[5] *humorous*] damp and inducing strange moods.
[6] *medlars . . . poperin pear*] the fruits are euphemisms for sexual organs.

Romeo, good night: I'll to my truckle-bed;[7]
This field-bed is too cold for me to sleep:
Come, shall we go?

BEN.   Go then, for 'tis in vain.
To seek him here that means not to be found.   [*Exeunt.*

SCENE II. *Capulet's orchard.*

Enter ROMEO.

ROM.   He jests at scars that never felt a wound.
                 [JULIET *appears above at a window.*
But, soft! what light through yonder window breaks?
It is the east, and Juliet is the sun!
Arise, fair sun, and kill the envious moon,
Who is already sick and pale with grief,
That thou her maid art far more fair than she:
Be not her maid, since she is envious;
Her vestal livery is but sick and green,
And none but fools do wear it; cast it off.
It is my lady; O, it is my love!
O, that she knew she were!
She speaks, yet she says nothing: what of that?
Her eye discourses, I will answer it.
I am too bold, 'tis not to me she speaks:
Two of the fairest stars in all the heaven,
Having some business, do intreat her eyes
To twinkle in their spheres till they return.
What if her eyes were there, they in her head?
The brightness of her cheek would shame those stars,
As daylight doth a lamp; her eyes in heaven
Would through the airy region stream so bright
That birds would sing and think it were not night.
See, how she leans her cheek upon her hand!
O, that I were a glove upon that hand,
That I might touch that cheek!

JUL.   Ay me!
ROM.   She speaks:

---

[7] *truckle-bed*] a bed on casters that could be pushed under another bed.

O, speak again, bright angel! for thou art
As glorious to this night, being o'er my head,
As is a winged messenger of heaven
Unto the white-upturned wondering eyes
Of mortals that fall back to gaze on him,
When he bestrides the lazy-pacing clouds
And sails upon the bosom of the air.

JUL.   O Romeo, Romeo! wherefore art thou Romeo?
Deny thy father and refuse thy name;
Or, if thou wilt not, be but sworn my love,
And I'll no longer be a Capulet.

ROM.   [*Aside*] Shall I hear more, or shall I speak at this?

JUL.   'Tis but thy name that is my enemy;
Thou art thyself, though not a Montague.
What's Montague? it is nor hand, nor foot,
Nor arm, nor face, nor any other part
Belonging to a man. O, be some other name!
What's in a name? that which we call a rose
By any other name would smell as sweet;
So Romeo would, were he not Romeo call'd,
Retain that dear perfection which he owes[1]
Without that title. Romeo, doff thy name,
And for thy name, which is no part of thee,
Take all myself.

ROM.   I take thee at thy word:
Call me but love, and I'll be new baptized;
Henceforth I never will be Romeo.

JUL.   What man art thou, that, thus bescreen'd in night,
So stumblest on my counsel?

ROM.   By a name
I know not how to tell thee who I am:
My name, dear saint, is hateful to myself,
Because it is an enemy to thee;
Had I it written, I would tear the word.

JUL.   My ears have yet not drunk a hundred words
Of thy tongue's uttering, yet I know the sound:
Art thou not Romeo, and a Montague?

ROM.   Neither, fair maid, if either thee dislike.

JUL.   How camest thou hither, tell me, and wherefore?

---

[1] owes] possesses.

            The orchard walls are high and hard to climb,
            And the place death, considering who thou art,
            If any of my kinsmen find thee here.
ROM.   With love's light wings did I o'er-perch these walls,
            For stony limits cannot hold love out:
            And what love can do, that dares love attempt;
            Therefore thy kinsmen are no let[2] to me.
JUL.   If they do see thee, they will murder thee.
ROM.   Alack, there lies more peril in thine eye
            Than twenty of their swords: look thou but sweet,
            And I am proof against their enmity.
JUL.   I would not for the world they saw thee here.
ROM.   I have night's cloak to hide me from their eyes;
            And but thou love me, let them find me here:
            My life were better ended by their hate,
            Than death prorogued,[3] wanting of thy love.
JUL.   By whose direction found'st thou out this place?
ROM.   By love, that first did prompt me to inquire;
            He lent me counsel, and I lent him eyes.
            I am no pilot; yet, wert thou as far
            As that vast shore wash'd with the farthest sea,
            I would adventure for such merchandise.
JUL.   Thou know'st the mask of night is on my face,
            Else would a maiden blush bepaint my cheek
            For that which thou hast heard me speak to-night.
            Fain would I dwell on form, fain, fain deny
            What I have spoke: but farewell compliment![4]
            Dost thou love me? I know thou wilt say 'Ay,'
            And I will take thy word: yet, if thou swear'st,
            Thou mayst prove false: at lovers' perjuries,
            They say, Jove laughs. O gentle Romeo,
            If thou dost love, pronounce it faithfully:
            Or if thou think'st I am too quickly won,
            I'll frown and be perverse and say thee nay,
            So thou wilt woo; but else, not for the world.
            In truth, fair Montague, I am too fond;[5]

---

[2] *let*] hindrance.
[3] *prorogued*] postponed.
[4] *compliment*] formality.
[5] *fond*] foolish.

And therefore thou mayst think my 'havior light:
But trust me, gentleman, I'll prove more true
Than those that have more cunning to be strange.[6]
I should have been more strange, I must confess,
But that thou overheard'st, ere I was ware,
My true love's passion: therefore pardon me,
And not impute this yielding to light love,
Which the dark night hath so discovered.

ROM.   Lady, by yonder blessed moon I swear,
     That tips with silver all these fruit-tree tops,—

JUL.   O, swear not by the moon, th' inconstant moon,
     That monthly changes in her circled orb,
     Lest that thy love prove likewise variable.

ROM.   What shall I swear by?

JUL.   Do not swear at all;
     Or, if thou wilt, swear by thy gracious self,
     Which is the god of my idolatry,
     And I'll believe thee.

ROM.   If my heart's dear love—

JUL.   Well, do not swear: although I joy in thee,
     I have no joy of this contract to-night:
     It is too rash, too unadvised, too sudden,
     Too like the lightning, which doth cease to be
     Ere one can say 'It lightens.' Sweet, good night!
     This bud of love, by summer's ripening breath,
     May prove a beauteous flower when next we meet.
     Good night, good night! as sweet repose and rest
     Come to thy heart as that within my breast!

ROM.   O, wilt thou leave me so unsatisfied?

JUL.   What satisfaction canst thou have to-night?

ROM.   The exchange of thy love's faithful vow for mine.

JUL.   I gave thee mine before thou didst request it:
     And yet I would it were to give again.

ROM.   Wouldst thou withdraw it? for what purpose, love?

JUL.   But to be frank,[7] and give it thee again.
     And yet I wish but for the thing I have:
     My bounty is as boundless as the sea,
     My love as deep; the more I give to thee,

---

[6] *strange*] reserved, distant.
[7] *frank*] bountiful.

The more I have, for both are infinite.
I hear some noise within; dear love, adieu! [NURSE *calls within.*
Anon, good Nurse! Sweet Montague, be true.
Stay but a little, I will come again.   [*Exit.*
ROM.   O blessed, blessed night! I am afeard,
    Being in night, all this is but a dream,
    Too flattering-sweet to be substantial.

Re-enter JULIET, *above.*

JUL.   Three words, dear Romeo, and good night indeed.
    If that thy bent of love be honourable,
    Thy purpose marriage, send me word to-morrow,
    By one that I'll procure to come to thee,
    Where and what time thou wilt perform the rite,
    And all my fortunes at thy foot I'll lay,
    And follow thee my lord throughout the world.
NURSE.   [*Within*] Madam!
JUL.   I come, anon.—But if thou mean'st not well,
    I do beseech thee—
NURSE.   [*Within*] Madam!
JUL.   By and by, I come:—
    To cease thy suit, and leave me to my grief:
    To-morrow will I send.
ROM.   So thrive my soul,—
JUL.   A thousand times good night!   [*Exit.*
ROM.   A thousand times the worse, to want thy light.
    Love goes toward love, as schoolboys from their books,
    But love from love, toward school with heavy looks. [*Retiring slowly.*

Re-enter JULIET, *above.*

JUL.   Hist! Romeo, hist!—O, for a falconer's voice,
    To lure this tassel-gentle[8] back again!
    Bondage is hoarse, and may not speak aloud;
    Else would I tear the cave where Echo lies,
    And make her airy tongue more hoarse than mine,
    With repetition of my Romeo's name.
    Romeo!
ROM.   It is my soul that calls upon my name:
    How silver-sweet sound lovers' tongues by night,
    Like softest music to attending ears!

---

[8] *tassel-gentle*] male goshawk.

JUL.   Romeo!
ROM.   My dear?
JUL.   At what o'clock to-morrow
        Shall I send to thee?
ROM.   At the hour of nine.
JUL.   I will not fail: 'tis twenty years till then.
        I have forgot why I did call thee back.
ROM.   Let me stand here till thou remember it.
JUL.   I shall forget, to have thee still stand there,
        Remembering how I love thy company.
ROM.   And I'll still stay, to have thee still forget,
        Forgetting any other home but this.
JUL.   'Tis almost morning; I would have thee gone:
        And yet no farther than a wanton's bird,
        Who lets it hop a little from her hand,
        Like a poor prisoner in his twisted gyves,
        And with a silk thread plucks it back again,
        So loving-jealous of his liberty.
ROM.   I would I were thy bird.
JUL.   Sweet, so would I:
        Yet I should kill thee with much cherishing.
        Good night, good night! parting is such sweet sorrow
        That I shall say good night till it be morrow.   [*Exit.*
ROM.   Sleep dwell upon thine eyes, peace in thy breast!
        Would I were sleep and peace, so sweet to rest!
        Hence will I to my ghostly[9] father's cell,
        His help to crave and my dear hap[10] to tell.   [*Exit.*

SCENE III. *Friar Laurence's cell.*

Enter FRIAR LAURENCE, *with a basket.*

FRI. L.   The grey-eyed morn smiles on the frowning night,
           Chequering the eastern clouds with streaks of light;
           And flecked darkness like a drunkard reels
           From forth day's path and Titan's[1] fiery wheels:
           Now, ere the sun advance his burning eye,

---

[9] *ghostly*] spiritual.
[10] *hap*] fortune.

---

[1] *Titan's*] the Titan Helios, god of the sun.

The day to cheer and night's dank dew to dry,
I must up-fill this osier cage of ours
With baleful weeds and precious-juiced flowers.
The earth that's nature's mother is her tomb;
What is her burying grave, that is her womb:
And from her womb children of divers kind
We sucking on her natural bosom find,
Many for many virtues excellent,
None but for some, and yet all different.
O, mickle[2] is the powerful grace that lies
In herbs, plants, stones, and their true qualities:
For nought so vile that on the earth doth live,
But to the earth some special good doth give;
Nor aught so good, but, strain'd from that fair use,
Revolts from true birth, stumbling on abuse:
Virtue itself turns vice, being misapplied,
And vice sometime 's by action dignified.
Within the infant rind of this small flower
Poison hath residence, and medicine power:
For this, being smelt, with that part cheers each part,
Being tasted, slays all senses with the heart.
Two such opposed kings encamp them still
In man as well as herbs, grace and rude will;
And where the worser is predominant,
Full soon the canker death eats up that plant.

Enter ROMEO.

ROM.   Good morrow, father.
FRI. L.   Benedicite!
What early tongue so sweet saluteth me?
Young son, it argues a distemper'd head
So soon to bid good morrow to thy bed:
Care keeps his watch in every old man's eye,
And where care lodges, sleep will never lie;
But where unbruised youth with unstuff'd brain
Doth couch his limbs, there golden sleep doth reign:
Therefore thy earliness doth me assure
Thou art up-roused by some distemperature;
Or if not so, then here I hit it right,
Our Romeo hath not been in bed to-night.

___

[2] *mickle*] great.

Rom.   That last is true; the sweeter rest was mine.

Fri. L.   God pardon sin! wast thou with Rosaline?

Rom.   With Rosaline, my ghostly father? no;
    I have forgot that name and that name's woe.

Fri. L.   That's my good son: but where hast thou been then?

Rom.   I'll tell thee ere thou ask it me again.
    I have been feasting with mine enemy;
    Where on a sudden one hath wounded me,
    That's by me wounded: both our remedies
    Within thy help and holy physic lies:
    I bear no hatred, blessed man, for, lo,
    My intercession likewise steads[3] my foe.

Fri. L.   Be plain, good son, and homely in thy drift;
    Riddling confession finds but riddling shrift.

Rom.   Then plainly know my heart's dear love is set
    On the fair daughter of rich Capulet:
    As mine on hers, so hers is set on mine;
    And all combined, save what thou must combine
    By holy marriage: when, and where, and how,
    We met, we woo'd and made exchange of vow,
    I'll tell thee as we pass; but this I pray,
    That thou consent to marry us to-day.

Fri. L.   Holy Saint Francis, what a change is here!
    Is Rosaline, that thou didst love so dear,
    So soon forsaken? young men's love then lies
    Not truly in their hearts, but in their eyes.
    Jesu Maria, what a deal of brine
    Hath wash'd thy sallow cheeks for Rosaline!
    How much salt water thrown away in waste,
    To season love, that of it doth not taste!
    The sun not yet thy sighs from heaven clears,
    Thy old groans ring yet in mine ancient ears;
    Lo, here upon thy cheek the stain doth sit
    Of an old tear that is not wash'd off yet:
    If e'er thou wast thyself and these woes thine,
    Thou and these woes were all for Rosaline:
    And art thou changed? pronounce this sentence then:
    Women may fall when there's no strength in men.

Rom.   Thou chid'st me oft for loving Rosaline.

---

[3] *steads*] benefits.

FRI. L.   For doting, not for loving, pupil mine.

ROM.   And bad'st me bury love.

FRI. L.   Not in a grave,
To lay one in, another out to have.

ROM.   I pray thee, chide not: she whom I love now
Doth grace for grace and love for love allow;
The other did not so.

FRI. L.   O, she knew well
Thy love did read by rote and could not spell.
But come, young waverer, come, go with me,
In one respect I'll thy assistant be;
For this alliance may so happy prove,
To turn your households' rancour to pure love.

ROM.   O, let us hence; I stand on sudden haste.

FRI. L.   Wisely and slow; they stumble that run fast.   [*Exeunt.*

SCENE IV. *A street.*

Enter BENVOLIO *and* MERCUTIO.

MER.   Where the devil should this Romeo be? Came he not home to-night?

BEN.   Not to his father's; I spoke with his man.

MER.   Ah, that same pale hard-hearted wench, that Rosaline,
Torments him so that he will sure run mad.

BEN.   Tybalt, the kinsman to old Capulet,
Hath sent a letter to his father's house.

MER.   A challenge, on my life.

BEN.   Romeo will answer it.

MER.   Any man that can write may answer a letter.

BEN.   Nay, he will answer the letter's master, how he dares, being dared.

MER.   Alas, poor Romeo, he is already dead! stabbed with a white wench's black eye; shot thorough[1] the ear with a love-song; the very pin[2] of his heart cleft with the blind bow-boy's butt-shaft:[3] and is he a man to encounter Tybalt?

BEN.   Why, what is Tybalt?

---

[1] *thorough*] through.

[2] *pin*] center, middle of a target.

[3] *butt-shaft*] barbless arrow.

MER.   More than prince of cats,[+] I can tell you. O, he's the courageous captain of compliments.[5] He fights as you sing prick-song,[6] keeps time, distance and proportion;[7] rests me his minim rest, one, two, and the third in your bosom: the very butcher of a silk button, a duellist, a duellist; a gentleman of the very first house,[8] of the first and second cause:[9] ah, the immortal passado! the punto reverso! the hai![10]

BEN.   The what?

MER.   The pox of such antic, lisping, affecting fantasticoes;[11] these new tuners of accents! 'By Jesu, a very good blade! a very tall[12] man! a very good whore!' Why, is not this a lamentable thing, grandsire, that we should be thus afflicted with these strange flies,[13] these fashion-mongers, these perdona-mi's, who stand so much on the new form that they cannot sit at ease on the old bench? O, their bones,[14] their bones!

Enter ROMEO.

BEN.   Here comes Romeo, here comes Romeo.

MER.   Without his roe, like a dried herring: O flesh, flesh, how art thou fishified! Now is he for the numbers that Petrarch flowed in: Laura to his lady was but a kitchen-wench; marry, she had a better love to be-rhyme her; Dido, a dowdy; Cleopatra, a gipsy; Helen and Hero, hildings[15] and harlots; Thisbe, a grey eye or so, but not to the purpose. Signior Romeo, bon jour! there's a French salutation to your French slop.[16] You gave us the counterfeit fairly last night.

ROM.   Good morrow to you both. What counterfeit did I give you?

MER.   The slip,[17] sir, the slip; can you not conceive?

ROM.   Pardon, good Mercutio, my business was great; and in such a case as mine a man may strain courtesy.

[+] *prince of cats*] The prince of cats in *Reynard the Fox* is named Tybert.

[5] *captain of compliments*] master of ceremony.

[6] *prick-song*] sheet music.

[7] *proportion*] rhythm.

[8] *house*] rank, fencing school.

[9] *cause*] i.e., to take up a quarrel.

[10] *passado . . . punto reverso . . . hai*] fencing terms: forward thrust; backhanded stroke; home thrust.

[11] *fantasticoes*] coxcombs.

[12] *tall*] valiant.

[13] *strange flies*] parasites.

[14] *bones*] French *bon* pronounced to create an English pun.

[15] *hildings*] wretches.

[16] *slop*] large trousers.

[17] *slip*] a counterfeit coin.

MER.   That's as much as to say, Such a case as yours constrains a man to
      bow in the hams.

ROM.   Meaning, to court'sy.

MER.   Thou hast most kindly hit it.

ROM.   A most courteous exposition.

MER.   Nay, I am the very pink of courtesy.

ROM.   Pink for flower.

MER.   Right.

ROM.   Why, then is my pump[18] well flowered.

MER.   Well said: follow me this jest now, till thou hast worn out thy
      pump, that, when the single sole of it is worn, the jest may remain,
      after the wearing, solely singular.

ROM.   O single-soled jest, solely singular for the singleness![19]

MER.   Come between us, good Benvolio; my wits faint.

ROM.   Switch and spurs, switch and spurs; or I'll cry a match.[20]

MER.   Nay, if thy wits run the wild-goose chase,[21] I have done; for thou
      hast more of the wild-goose in one of thy wits than, I am sure, I have
      in my whole five: was I with you there for the goose?

ROM.   Thou wast never with me for any thing when thou wast not there
      for the goose.[22]

MER.   I will bite thee by the ear for that jest.

ROM.   Nay, good goose, bite not.

MER.   Thy wit is a very bitter sweeting;[23] it is a most sharp sauce.

ROM.   And is it not well served in to a sweet goose?

MER.   O, here's a wit of cheveril,[24] that stretches from an inch narrow
      to an ell broad!

ROM.   I stretch it out for that word 'broad'; which added to the goose,
      proves thee far and wide a broad goose.

MER.   Why, is not this better now than groaning for love? now art thou
      sociable, now art thou Romeo; now art thou what thou art, by art as
      well as by nature: for this drivelling love is like a great natural,[25] that
      runs lolling up and down to hide his bauble[26] in a hole.

BEN.   Stop there, stop there.

---

[18] *pump*] a light shoe (often decorated with ribbons shaped as flowers).

[19] *singleness*] silliness.

[20] *cry a match*] claim victory.

[21] *wild-goose chase*] a horse race in which the leader chooses whatever course he wishes.

[22] *goose*] prostitute.

[23] *sweeting*] apple sauce.

[24] *cheveril*] kid leather.

[25] *natural*] idiot, fool.

[26] *bauble*] the fool's club, here with a bawdy quibble.

MER.   Thou desirest me to stop in my tale against the hair.[27]

BEN.   Thou wouldst else have made thy tale large.

MER.   O, thou art deceived; I would have made it short: for I was come
        to the whole depth of my tale, and meant indeed to occupy the
        argument no longer.

ROM.   Here's goodly gear!

Enter NURSE *and* PETER.

MER.   A sail, a sail!

BEN.   Two, two; a shirt and a smock.[28]

NURSE. Peter!

PETER. Anon.

NURSE. My fan, Peter.

MER.   Good Peter, to hide her face; for her fan's the fairer of the two.

NURSE. God ye good morrow, gentlemen.

MER.   God ye good den, fair gentlewoman.

NURSE. Is it good den?

MER.   'Tis no less, I tell you; for the bawdy hand of the dial is now upon
        the prick of noon.

NURSE. Out upon you! what a man[29] are you?

ROM.   One, gentlewoman, that God hath made himself to mar.

NURSE. By my troth, it is well said; 'for himself to mar,' quoth a'?
        Gentlemen, can any of you tell me where I may find the young
        Romeo?

ROM.   I can tell you; but young Romeo will be older when you have
        found him than he was when you sought him: I am the youngest of
        that name, for fault of a worse.

NURSE. You say well.

MER.   Yea, is the worst well? very well took, i' faith; wisely, wisely.

NURSE. If you be he, sir, I desire some confidence[30] with you.

BEN.   She will indite[31] him to some supper.

MER.   A bawd, a bawd, a bawd! So ho!

ROM.   What hast thou found?

MER.   No hare, sir; unless a hare, sir, in a lenten pie, that is something
        stale and hoar[32] ere it be spent.   [*Sings.*

---

[27] *against the hair*] against the grain, with quibbling.

[28] *a shirt . . . smock*] i.e., a man and a woman.

[29] *what a man*] what sort of a man.

[30] *confidence*] the Nurse's malapropism for "conference."

[31] *indite*] a deliberate malapropism for "invite."

[32] *hoar*] moldy, punning on "whore."

An old hare hoar,
And an old hare hoar,
Is very good meat in lent:
But a hare that is hoar,
Is too much for a score,
When it hoars ere it be spent.

Romeo, will you come to your father's? we'll to dinner thither.

ROM.   I will follow you.

MER.   Farewell, ancient lady; farewell, [*singing*] 'lady, lady, lady.'

[*Exeunt* MERCUTIO *and* BENVOLIO.

NURSE.   Marry, farewell! I pray you, sir, what saucy merchant[33] was this, that was so full of his ropery?[34]

ROM.   A gentleman, nurse, that loves to hear himself talk, and will speak more in a minute than he will stand to in a month.

NURSE.   An a' speak any thing against me, I'll take him down, an a' were lustier than he is, and twenty such Jacks;[35] and if I cannot, I'll find those that shall. Scurvy knave! I am none of his flirt-gills;[36] I am none of his skains-mates.[37] [*Turning to* PETER] And thou must stand by too, and suffer every knave to use me at his pleasure?

PETER.   I saw no man use you at his pleasure; if I had, my weapon should quickly have been out, I warrant you: I dare draw as soon as another man, if I see occasion in a good quarrel and the law on my side.

NURSE.   Now, afore God, I am so vexed that every part about me quivers. Scurvy knave! Pray you, sir, a word: and as I told you, my young lady bade me inquire you out; what she bade me say, I will keep to myself: but first let me tell ye, if ye should lead her into a fool's paradise, as they say, it were a very gross kind of behaviour, as they say: for the gentlewoman is young, and therefore, if you should deal double with her, truly it were an ill thing to be offered to any gentlewoman, and very weak[38] dealing.

ROM.   Nurse, commend me to thy lady and mistress. I protest unto thee—

---

[33] *merchant*] fellow.
[34] *ropery*] malapropism for "roguery."
[35] *Jacks*] term of contempt for an impudent fellow.
[36] *flirt-gills*] loose women.
[37] *skains-mates*] cutthroats.
[38] *weak*] contemptible.

NURSE.   Good heart, and, i' faith, I will tell her as much: Lord, Lord, she will be a joyful woman.

ROM.   What wilt thou tell her, Nurse? thou dost not mark me.

NURSE.   I will tell her, sir, that you do protest; which, as I take it, is a gentlemanlike offer.

ROM.   Bid her devise
Some means to come to shrift this afternoon;
And there she shall at Friar Laurence' cell
Be shrived and married. Here is for thy pains.

NURSE.   No, truly, sir; not a penny.

ROM.   Go to; I say you shall.

NURSE.   This afternoon, sir? well, she shall be there.

ROM.   And stay, good nurse, behind the abbey-wall:
Within this hour my man shall be with thee,
And bring thee cords made like a tackled stair;[39]
Which to the high top-gallant of my joy
Must be my convoy in the secret night.
Farewell; be trusty, and I'll quit[40] thy pains:
Farewell; commend me to thy mistress.

NURSE.   Now God in heaven bless thee! Hark you, sir.

ROM.   What say'st thou, my dear nurse?

NURSE.   Is your man secret? Did you ne'er hear say,
      Two may keep counsel, putting one away?

ROM.   I warrant thee, my man's as true as steel.

NURSE.   Well, sir; my mistress is the sweetest lady—Lord, Lord! when 'twas a little prating thing—O, there is a nobleman in town, one Paris, that would fain lay knife aboard; but she, good soul, had as lieve see a toad, a very toad, as see him. I anger her sometimes, and tell her that Paris is the properer man; but, I'll warrant you, when I say so, she looks as pale as any clout[41] in the versal[42] world. Doth not rosemary and Romeo begin both with a[43] letter?

ROM.   Ay, nurse; what of that? both with an R.

NURSE.   Ah, mocker! that's the dog's name; R is for the—No; I know it begins with some other letter—and she hath the prettiest sententious[44] of it, of you and rosemary, that it would do you good to hear it.

---

[39] *tackled stair*] rope ladder.

[40] *quit*] reward.

[41] *clout*] piece of cloth.

[42] *versal*] universal, whole.

[43] *a*] one and the same.

[44] *sententious*] a malapropism, probably for "sentence," pithy saying.

ROM.   Commend me to thy lady.
NURSE.   Ay, a thousand times. [*Exit* ROMEO.] Peter!
PET.   Anon.
NURSE.   Peter, take my fan, and go before, and apace.   [*Exeunt.*

SCENE V. *Capulet's orchard.*

Enter JULIET.

JUL.   The clock struck nine when I did send the Nurse;
     In half an hour she promised to return.
     Perchance she cannot meet him: that's not so.
     O, she is lame! love's heralds should be thoughts,
     Which ten times faster glide than the sun's beams,
     Driving back shadows over louring hills:
     Therefore do nimble-pinion'd doves draw love,[1]
     And therefore hath the wind-swift Cupid wings.
     Now is the sun upon the highmost hill
     Of this day's journey, and from nine till twelve
     Is three long hours; yet she is not come.
     Had she affections and warm youthful blood,
     She would be as swift in motion as a ball;
     My words would bandy[2] her to my sweet love,
     And his to me:
     But old folks, many feign as they were dead;
     Unwieldy, slow, heavy and pale as lead.

Enter NURSE, *with* PETER.

     O God, she comes! O honey Nurse, what news?
     Hast thou met with him? Send thy man away.
NURSE.   Peter, stay at the gate.   [*Exit* PETER.
JUL.   Now, good sweet Nurse,—O Lord, why look'st thou sad?
     Though news be sad, yet tell them merrily;
     If good, thou shamest the music of sweet news
     By playing it to me with so sour a face.
NURSE.   I am a-weary; give me leave a while.
     Fie how my bones ache! what a jaunce[3] have I had!

---

[1] *love*] Venus, goddess of love, whose chariot was drawn by doves.
[2] *bandy*] strike (as a ball).
[3] *jaunce*] hard journey.

JUL.   I would thou hadst my bones and I thy news:
       Nay, come, I pray thee, speak; good, good Nurse, speak.
NURSE.   Jesu, what haste? can you not stay a while?
       Do you not see that I am out of breath?
JUL.   How art thou out of breath, when thou hast breath
       To say to me that thou art out of breath?
       The excuse that thou dost make in this delay
       Is longer than the tale thou dost excuse.
       Is thy news good, or bad? answer to that;
       Say either, and I'll stay the circumstance:+
       Let me be satisfied, is't good or bad?
NURSE.   Well, you have made a simple choice; you know not how to
       choose a man: Romeo! no, not he; though his face be better than
       any man's, yet his leg excels all men's; and for a hand, and a foot,
       and a body, though they be not to be talked on, yet they are past
       compare: he is not the flower of courtesy, but, I'll warrant him, as
       gentle as a lamb. Go thy ways, wench; serve God. What, have you
       dined at home?
JUL.   No, no: but all this did I know before.
       What says he of our marriage? what of that?
NURSE.   Lord, how my head aches! what a head have I!
       It beats as it would fall in twenty pieces.
       My back o' t' other side,—ah, my back, my back!
       Beshrew your heart for sending me about,
       To catch my death with jauncing up and down!
JUL.   I' faith, I am sorry that thou art not well.
       Sweet, sweet, sweet Nurse, tell me, what says my love?
NURSE.   Your love says, like an honest gentleman, and a courteous, and
       a kind, and a handsome, and, I warrant, a virtuous,—Where is
       your mother?
JUL.   Where is my mother! why, she is within;
       Where should she be? How oddly thou repliest!
       'Your love says, like an honest gentleman,
       Where is your mother?'
NURSE.   O God's lady dear!
       Are you so hot? marry, come up, I trow;
       Is this the poultice for my aching bones?
       Henceforward do your messages yourself.

+ *stay the circumstance*] wait until later for the details.

JUL.   Here's such a coil![5] come, what says Romeo?
NURSE.   Have you got leave to go to shrift to-day?
JUL.   I have.
NURSE.   Then hie you hence to Friar Laurence' cell;
  There stays a husband to make you a wife:
  Now comes the wanton blood up in your cheeks,
  They'll be in scarlet straight at any news.
  Hie you to church; I must another way,
  To fetch a ladder, by the which your love
  Must climb a bird's nest soon when it is dark;
  I am the drudge, and toil in your delight;
  But you shall bear the burthen soon at night.
  Go; I'll to dinner; hie you to the cell.
JUL.   Hie to high fortune! Honest Nurse, farewell.   [*Exeunt.*

SCENE VI. *Friar Laurence's cell.*

Enter FRIAR LAURENCE *and* ROMEO.

FRI. L.   So smile the heavens upon this holy act
  That after-hours with sorrow chide us not!
ROM.   Amen, amen! but come what sorrow can,
  It cannot countervail[1] the exchange of joy
  That one short minute gives me in her sight:
  Do thou but close our hands with holy words,
  Then love-devouring death do what he dare,
  It is enough I may but call her mine.
FRI. L.   These violent delights have violent ends,
  And in their triumph die; like fire and powder
  Which as they kiss consume: the sweetest honey
  Is loathsome in his own deliciousness,
  And in the taste confounds[2] the appetite:
  Therefore, love moderately; long love doth so;
  Too swift arrives as tardy as too slow.

Enter JULIET.

[5] *coil*] turmoil, confusion.

[1] *countervail*] equal.
[2] *confounds*] destroys, does away with.

Here comes the lady. O, so light a foot
Will ne'er wear out the everlasting flint.
A lover may bestride the gossamer
That idles in the wanton summer air,
And yet not fall; so light is vanity.

JUL.   Good even to my ghostly confessor.

FRI. L.   Romeo shall thank thee, daughter, for us both.

JUL.   As much to him, else is his thanks too much.

ROM.   Ah, Juliet, if the measure of thy joy
Be heap'd like mine, and that thy skill be more
To blazon it, then sweeten with thy breath
This neighbour air, and let rich music's tongue
Unfold the imagined happiness that both
Receive in either by this dear encounter.

JUL.   Conceit,[3] more rich in matter than in words,
Brags of his substance, not of ornament:
They are but beggars that can count their worth;
But my true love is grown to such excess,
I cannot sum up sum of half my wealth.

FRI. L.   Come, come with me, and we will make short work;
For, by your leaves, you shall not stay alone
Till holy church incorporate two in one.   [*Exeunt.*

[3] *Conceit*] Imagination.

ACT III.

SCENE I. A *public place*.

Enter MERCUTIO, BENVOLIO, Page, *and* Servants.

BEN. I pray thee, good Mercutio, let's retire:
    The day is hot, the Capulets abroad,
    And, if we meet, we shall not 'scape a brawl;
    For now these hot days is the mad blood stirring.

MER. Thou art like one of those fellows that when he enters the confines of a tavern claps me his sword upon the table, and says 'God send me no need of thee!' and by the operation of the second cup draws it on the drawer,[1] when indeed there is no need.

BEN. Am I like such a fellow?

MER. Come, come, thou art as hot a Jack in thy mood as any in Italy, and as soon moved to be moody,[2] and as soon moody to be moved.

BEN. And what to?

MER. Nay, an there were two such, we should have none shortly, for one would kill the other. Thou! why, thou wilt quarrel with a man that hath a hair more, or a hair less, in his beard than thou hast: thou wilt quarrel with a man for cracking nuts, having no other reason but because thou hast hazel eyes; what eye, but such an eye, would spy out such a quarrel? thy head is as full of quarrels as an egg is full of meat, and yet thy head hath been beaten as addle as an egg for quarrelling: thou hast quarrelled with a man for coughing in the street, because he hath wakened thy dog that hath lain asleep in the sun: didst thou not fall out with a tailor for wearing his new doublet before Easter? with another, for tying his new shoes with old riband? and yet thou wilt tutor me from quarrelling!

---

[1] *drawer*] waiter.
[2] *moody*] angry.

43

BEN.   An I were so apt to quarrel as thou art, any man should buy the
        fee-simple of my life for an hour and a quarter.
MER.   The fee-simple! O simple!

Enter TYBALT *and others.*

BEN.   By my head, here come the Capulets.
MER.   By my heel, I care not.
TYB.   Follow me close, for I will speak to them.
        Gentlemen, good den: a word with one of you.
MER.   And but one word with one of us? couple it with something;
        make it a word and a blow.
TYB.   You shall find me apt enough to that, sir, an you will give me
        occasion.
MER.   Could you not take some occasion without giving?
TYB.   Mercutio, thou consort'st with Romeo,—
MER.   Consort! what, dost thou make us minstrels? an thou make
        minstrels of us, look to hear nothing but discords: here's my fid-
        dlestick; here's that shall make you dance. 'Zounds, consort!
BEN.   We talk here in the public haunt of men:
        Either withdraw unto some private place,
        Or reason coldly of your grievances,
        Or else depart; here all eyes gaze on us.
MER.   Men's eyes were made to look, and let them gaze;
        I will not budge for no man's pleasure, I.

Enter ROMEO.

TYB.   Well, peace be with you, sir: here comes my man.
MER.   But I'll be hang'd, sir, if he wear your livery:
        Marry, go before to field, he'll be your follower;
        Your worship in that sense may call him man.
TYB.   Romeo, the love I bear thee can afford
        No better term than this,—thou art a villain.
ROM.   Tybalt, the reason that I have to love thee
        Doth much excuse the appertaining rage
        To such a greeting: villain am I none;
        Therefore farewell; I see thou know'st me not.
TYB.   Boy, this shall not excuse the injuries
        That thou hast done me; therefore turn and draw.
ROM.   I do protest, I never injured thee,
        But love thee better than thou canst devise
        Till thou shalt know the reason of my love:

And so, good Capulet,—which name I tender
As dearly as mine own,—be satisfied.

MER.   O calm, dishonourable, vile submission!
Alla stoccata[3] carries it away.   [*Draws.*
Tybalt, you rat-catcher, will you walk?

TYB.   What wouldst thou have with me?

MER.   Good king of cats, nothing but one of your nine lives, that I
mean to make bold withal, and, as you shall use me hereafter, dry-
beat[4] the rest of the eight. Will you pluck your sword out of his
pilcher[5] by the ears? make haste, lest mine be about your ears ere it
be out.

TYB.   I am for you.   [*Drawing.*

ROM.   Gentle Mercutio, put thy rapier up.

MER.   Come, sir, your passado.   [*They fight.*

ROM.   Draw, Benvolio; beat down their weapons.
Gentlemen, for shame, forbear this outrage!
Tybalt, Mercutio, the prince expressly hath
Forbid this bandying in Verona streets:
Hold, Tybalt! good Mercutio!
[TYBALT *under* ROMEO'S *arm stabs* MERCUTIO *and*
                                         flies with his followers.

MER.   I am hurt;
A plague o' both your houses! I am sped:[6]
Is he gone, and hath nothing?

BEN.   What, art thou hurt?

MER.   Ay, ay, a scratch, a scratch; marry, 'tis enough.
Where is my page? Go, villain, fetch a surgeon.   [*Exit* Page.

ROM.   Courage, man; the hurt cannot be much.

MER.   No, 'tis not so deep as a well, nor so wide as a church-door; but
'tis enough, 'twill serve: ask for me to-morrow, and you shall find me
a grave man. I am peppered, I warrant, for this world. A plague o'
both your houses! 'Zounds, a dog, a rat, a mouse, a cat, to scratch a
man to death! a braggart, a rogue, a villain, that fights by the book
of arithmetic![7] Why the devil came you between us? I was hurt
under your arm.

ROM.   I thought all for the best.

---

[3] *Alla stoccata*] a technical term for a fencing thrust.
[4] *dry-beat*] cudgel.
[5] *pilcher*] scabbard.
[6] *sped*] done for.
[7] *book of arithmetic*] fencing manual.

MER.   Help me into some house, Benvolio,
        Or I shall faint. A plague o' both your houses!
        They have made worms' meat of me: I have it,
        And soundly too: your houses!

                            [*Exeunt* MERCUTIO *and* BENVOLIO.

ROM.   This gentleman, the Prince's near ally,[8]
        My very friend, hath got this mortal hurt
        In my behalf; my reputation stain'd
        With Tybalt's slander,—Tybalt, that an hour
        Hath been my kinsman: O sweet Juliet,
        Thy beauty hath made me effeminate,
        And in my temper soften'd valour's steel!

Re-enter BENVOLIO.

BEN.   O Romeo, Romeo, brave Mercutio's dead!
        That gallant spirit hath aspired the clouds,
        Which too untimely here did scorn the earth.
ROM.   This day's black fate on more days doth depend;
        This but begins the woe others must end.

Re-enter TYBALT.

BEN.   Here comes the furious Tybalt back again.
ROM.   Alive, in triumph! and Mercutio slain!
        Away to heaven, respective lenity,[9]
        And fire-eyed fury be my conduct[10] now!
        Now, Tybalt, take the 'villain' back again
        That late thou gavest me; for Mercutio's soul
        Is but a little way above our heads,
        Staying for thine to keep him company:
        Either thou, or I, or both, must go with him.
TYB.   Thou, wretched boy, that didst consort him here,
        Shalt with him hence.
Rom.   This shall determine that.

                            [*They fight*; TYBALT *falls*.

BEN.   Romeo, away, be gone!
        The citizens are up, and Tybalt slain:
        Stand not amazed: the Prince will doom thee death
        If thou art taken: hence, be gone, away!

    [8] *ally*] relative.
    [9] *respective lenity*] concern for mildness.
    [10] *conduct*] guide.

ROM.   O, I am fortune's fool!
BEN.   Why dost thou stay?   [*Exit* ROMEO.

Enter Citizens, &c.

FIRST CIT.   Which way ran he that kill'd Mercutio?
     Tybalt, that murderer, which way ran he?
BEN.   There lies that Tybalt.
FIRST CIT.   Up, sir, go with me;
     I charge thee in the Prince's name, obey.

Enter PRINCE, *attended*; MONTAGUE, CAPULET, *their* Wives, *and others*.

PRIN.   Where are the vile beginners of this fray?
BEN.   O noble Prince, I can discover[11] all
     The unlucky manage of this fatal brawl:
     There lies the man, slain by young Romeo,
     That slew thy kinsman, brave Mercutio.
LA. CAP.   Tybalt, my cousin! O my brother's child!
     O Prince! O cousin! husband! O, the blood is spilt
     Of my dear kinsman! Prince, as thou art true,
     For blood of ours, shed blood of Montague.
     O cousin, cousin!
PRIN.   Benvolio, who began this bloody fray?
BEN.   Tybalt, here slain, whom Romeo's hand did slay;
     Romeo that spoke him fair, bid him bethink
     How nice[12] the quarrel was, and urged withal
     Your high displeasure: all this uttered
     With gentle breath, calm look, knees humbly bow'd,
     Could not take truce with the unruly spleen[13]
     Of Tybalt deaf to peace, but that he tilts
     With piercing steel at bold Mercutio's breast;
     Who, all as hot, turns deadly point to point,
     And, with a martial scorn, with one hand beats
     Cold death aside, and with the other sends
     It back to Tybalt, whose dexterity
     Retorts it: Romeo he cries aloud,
     'Hold, friends! friends, part!' and, swifter than his tongue,
     His agile arm beats down their fatal points,

[11] *discover*] reveal.
[12] *nice*] trivial.
[13] *take . . . spleen*] make peace with the uncontrollable rage.

And 'twixt them rushes; underneath whose arm
An envious thrust from Tybalt hit the life
Of stout Mercutio, and then Tybalt fled:
But by and by comes back to Romeo,
Who had but newly entertain'd revenge,
And to't they go like lightning: for, ere I
Could draw to part them, was stout Tybalt slain;
And, as he fell, did Romeo turn and fly;
This is the truth, or let Benvolio die.

LA. CAP.   He is a kinsman to the Montague,
Affection makes him false, he speaks not true:
Some twenty of them fought in this black strife,
And all those twenty could but kill one life.
I beg for justice, which thou, Prince, must give;
Romeo slew Tybalt, Romeo must not live.

PRIN.   Romeo slew him, he slew Mercutio;
Who now the price of his dear blood doth owe?

MON.   Not Romeo, Prince, he was Mercutio's friend;
His fault concludes but what the law should end,
The life of Tybalt.

PRIN.   And for that offence
Immediately we do exile him hence:
I have an interest in your hate's proceeding,
My blood for your rude brawls doth lie a-bleeding;
But I'll amerce[14] you with so strong a fine,
That you shall all repent the loss of mine:
I will be deaf to pleading and excuses;
Nor tears nor prayers shall purchase out abuses:[15]
Therefore use none: let Romeo hence in haste,
Else, when he's found, that hour is his last.
Bear hence this body, and attend our will:
Mercy but murders, pardoning those that kill.   [*Exeunt*.

---

[14] *amerce*] punish by imposing a fine.
[15] *purchase out abuses*] buy off the fine for misdeeds.

SCENE II. *Capulet's orchard.*

Enter JULIET.

JUL.   Gallop apace, you fiery-footed steeds,
          Towards Phoebus' lodging: such a waggoner
          As Phaethon would whip you to the west,
          And bring in cloudy night immediately.
          Spread thy close curtain, love-performing night,
          That runaways' eyes may wink, and Romeo
          Leap to these arms, untalk'd of and unseen.
          Lovers can see to do their amorous rites
          By their own beauties; or, if love be blind,
          It best agrees with night. Come, civil night,
          Thou sober-suited matron, all in black,
          And learn me how to lose a winning match,
          Play'd for a pair of stainless maidenhoods:
          Hood my unmann'd[1] blood bating in my cheeks
          With thy black mantle, till strange love grown bold
          Think true love acted simple modesty.
          Come, night, come, Romeo, come, thou day in night;
          For thou wilt lie upon the wings of night
          Whiter than new snow on a raven's back.
          Come, gentle night, come, loving, black-brow'd night,
          Give me my Romeo; and, when he shall die,
          Take him and cut him out in little stars,
          And he will make the face of heaven so fine,
          That all the world will be in love with night,
          And pay no worship to the garish sun.
          O, I have bought the mansion of a love,
          But not possess'd it, and, though I am sold,
          Not yet enjoy'd; so tedious is this day
          As is the night before some festival
          To an impatient child that hath new robes
          And may not wear them. O, here comes my Nurse,
          And she brings news, and every tongue that speaks
          But Romeo's name speaks heavenly eloquence.

---

[1] *unmann'd*] (1) untrained; (2) still without husband.

Enter NURSE, *with cords.*

    Now, Nurse, what news? What hast thou there? the cords
    That Romeo bid thee fetch?
NURSE.   Ay, ay, the cords. [*Throws them down.*
JUL.   Ay me! what news? why dost thou wring thy hands?
NURSE.   Ah, well-a-day! he's dead, he's dead, he's dead.
    We are undone, lady, we are undone.
    Alack the day! he's gone, he's kill'd, he's dead.
JUL.   Can heaven be so envious?
NURSE.   Romeo can,
    Though heaven cannot. O Romeo, Romeo!
    Who ever would have thought it? Romeo!
JUL.   What devil art thou that dost torment me thus?
    This torture should be roar'd in dismal hell.
    Hath Romeo slain himself? say thou but 'I,'[2]
    And that bare vowel 'I' shall poison more
    Than the death-darting eye of cockatrice:
    I am not I, if there be such an I,
    Or those eyes shut, that make thee answer 'I.'
    If he be slain, say 'I'; or if not, no:
    Brief sounds determine of my weal or woe.
NURSE.   I saw the wound, I saw it with mine eyes—
    God save the mark!—here on his manly breast:
    A piteous corse, a bloody piteous corse;
    Pale, pale as ashes, all bedaub'd in blood,
    All in gore[3] blood: I swounded at the sight.
JUL.   O, break, my heart! poor bankrupt, break at once!
    To prison, eyes, ne'er look on liberty!
    Vile earth, to earth resign, end motion here,
    And thou and Romeo press one heavy bier!
NURSE.   O Tybalt, Tybalt, the best friend I had!
    O courteous Tybalt! honest gentleman!
    That ever I should live to see thee dead!
JUL.   What storm is this that blows so contrary?
    Is Romeo slaughter'd, and is Tybalt dead?
    My dear-loved cousin, and my dearer lord?
    Then, dreadful trumpet, sound the general doom!
    For who is living, if those two are gone?

---

[2] 'I'] ay, yes.
[3] gore] clotted.

NURSE.   Tybalt is gone, and Romeo banished;
    Romeo that kill'd him, he is banished.
JUL.   O God! did Romeo's hand shed Tybalt's blood?
NURSE.   It did, it did; alas the day, it did!
JUL.   O serpent heart, hid with a flowering face!
    Did ever dragon keep so fair a cave?
    Beautiful tyrant! fiend angelical!
    Dove-feather'd raven! wolvish-ravening lamb!
    Despised substance of divinest show!
    Just opposite to what thou justly seem'st,
    A damned saint, an honourable villain!
    O nature, what hadst thou to do in hell,
    When thou didst bower the spirit of a fiend
    In mortal paradise of such sweet flesh?
    Was ever book containing such vile matter
    So fairly bound? O, that deceit should dwell
    In such a gorgeous palace!
NURSE.   There's no trust,
    No faith, no honesty in men; all perjured,
    All forsworn, all naught,[4] all dissemblers.
    Ah, where's my man? give me some aqua vitae:
    These griefs, these woes, these sorrows make me old.
    Shame come to Romeo!
JUL.   Blister'd be thy tongue
    For such a wish! he was not born to shame:
    Upon his brow shame is ashamed to sit;
    For 'tis a throne where honour may be crown'd
    Sole monarch of the universal earth.
    O, what a beast was I to chide at him!
NURSE.   Will you speak well of him that kill'd your cousin?
JUL.   Shall I speak ill of him that is my husband?
    Ah, poor my lord, what tongue shall smooth thy name,
    When I, thy three-hours wife, have mangled it?
    But wherefore, villain, didst thou kill my cousin?
    That villain cousin would have kill'd my husband:
    Back, foolish tears, back to your native spring;
    Your tributary drops belong to woe,
    Which you mistaking offer up to joy.
    My husband lives, that Tybalt would have slain;

---

[4] *naught*] worthless, wicked.

And Tybalt's dead, that would have slain my husband:
All this is comfort; wherefore weep I then?
Some word there was, worser than Tybalt's death,
That murder'd me: I would forget it fain;
But, O, it presses to my memory,
Like damned guilty deeds to sinners' minds:
'Tybalt is dead, and Romeo banished';
That 'banished,' that one word 'banished,'
Hath slain ten thousand Tybalts. Tybalt's death
Was woe enough, if it had ended there:
Or, if sour woe delights in fellowship,
And needly[5] will be rank'd with other griefs,
Why follow'd not, when she said 'Tybalt's dead,'
Thy father, or thy mother, nay, or both,
Which modern[6] lamentation might have moved?
But with a rear-ward[7] following Tybalt's death,
'Romeo is banished': to speak that word,
Is father, mother, Tybalt, Romeo, Juliet,
All slain, all dead. 'Romeo is banished.'
There is no end, no limit, measure, bound,
In that word's death; no words can that woe sound.
Where is my father, and my mother, Nurse?

NURSE.   Weeping and wailing over Tybalt's corse:
Will you go to them? I will bring you thither.

JUL.   Wash they his wounds with tears: mine shall be spent,
When theirs are dry, for Romeo's banishment.
Take up those cords: poor ropes, you are beguiled,
Both you and I; for Romeo is exiled:
He made you for a highway to my bed;
But I, a maid, die maiden-widowed.
Come, cords; come, Nurse; I'll to my wedding-bed;
And death, not Romeo, take my maidenhead!

NURSE.   Hie to your chamber: I'll find Romeo
To comfort you: I wot[8] well where he is.
Hark ye, your Romeo will be here at night:
I'll to him; he is hid at Laurence' cell.

JUL.   O, find him! give this ring to my true knight,
And bid him come to take his last farewell.   [*Exeunt.*

---

[5] *needly*] necessarily.
[6] *modern*] commonplace, ordinary.
[7] *rear-ward*] rear guard.
[8] *wot*] know.

SCENE III. *Friar Laurence's cell.*

Enter FRIAR LAURENCE.

FRI. L.   Romeo, come forth; come forth, thou fearful man:
  Affliction is enamour'd of thy parts,
  And thou art wedded to calamity.

Enter ROMEO.

ROM.   Father, what news? what is the Prince's doom?
  What sorrow craves acquaintance at my hand,
  That I yet know not?
FRI. L.   Too familiar
  Is my dear son with such sour company:
  I bring thee tidings of the Prince's doom.
ROM.   What less than dooms-day is the Prince's doom?
FRI. L.   A gentler judgement vanish'd[1] from his lips,
  Not body's death, but body's banishment.
ROM.   Ha, banishment! be merciful, say 'death';
  For exile hath more terror in his look,
  Much more than death: do not say 'banishment.'
FRI. L.   Here from Verona art thou banished:
  Be patient, for the world is broad and wide.
ROM.   There is no world without Verona walls,
  But purgatory, torture, hell itself.
  Hence banished is banish'd from the world,
  And world's exile is death: then 'banished'
  Is death mis-term'd: calling death 'banished,'
  Thou cut'st my head off with a golden axe,
  And smilest upon the stroke that murders me.
FRI. L.   O deadly sin! O rude unthankfulness!
  Thy fault our law calls death; but the kind Prince,
  Taking thy part, hath rush'd[2] aside the law,
  And turn'd that black word death to banishment:
  This is dear mercy, and thou seest it not.
ROM.   'Tis torture, and not mercy: heaven is here,
  Where Juliet lives; and every cat and dog

---

[1] *vanish'd*] issued.
[2] *rush'd*] violently thrust.

And little mouse, every unworthy thing,
Live here in heaven and may look on her,
But Romeo may not: more validity,[3]
More honourable state,[4] more courtship[5] lives
In carrion-flies than Romeo: they may seize
On the white wonder of dear Juliet's hand,
And steal immortal blessing from her lips;
Who, even in pure and vestal modesty,
Still blush, as thinking their own kisses sin;
But Romeo may not; he is banished:
This may flies do, but I from this must fly:
They are free men, but I am banished:
And say'st thou yet, that exile is not death?
Hadst thou no poison mix'd, no sharp-ground knife,
No sudden mean of death, though ne'er so mean,
But 'banished' to kill me?—'Banished'?
O Friar, the damned use that word in hell;
Howling attends it: how hast thou the heart,
Being a divine, a ghostly confessor,
A sin-absolver, and my friend profess'd,
To mangle me with that word 'banished'?

FRI. L.   Thou fond mad man, hear me but speak a word.

ROM.   O, thou wilt speak again of banishment.

FRI. L.   I'll give thee armour to keep off that word;
Adversity's sweet milk, philosophy,
To comfort thee, though thou art banished.

ROM.   Yet 'banished'? Hang up philosophy!
Unless philosophy can make a Juliet,
Displant a town, reverse a prince's doom,
It helps not, it prevails not: talk no more.

FRI. L.   O, then I see that madmen have no ears.

ROM.   How should they, when that wise men have no eyes?

FRI. L.   Let me dispute with thee of thy estate.[6]

ROM.   Thou canst not speak of that thou dost not feel:
Wert thou as young as I, Juliet thy love,
An hour but married, Tybalt murdered,
Doting like me, and like me banished,

---

[3] *validity*] value.
[4] *state*] rank.
[5] *courtship*] (1) civility befitting a courtier; (2) wooing.
[6] *dispute . . . estate*] discuss your situation with you.

    Then mightst thou speak, then mightst thou tear thy hair,
    And fall upon the ground, as I do now,
    Taking the measure of an unmade grave.   [*Knocking within.*

FRI. L.   Arise; one knocks; good Romeo, hide thyself.

ROM.   Not I; unless the breath of heart-sick groans
    Mist-like infold me from the search of eyes.   [*Knocking.*

FRI. L.   Hark, how they knock! Who's there? Romeo, arise;
    Thou wilt be taken.—Stay awhile!—Stand up;   [*Knocking.*
    Run to my study.—By and by!—God's will,
    What simpleness is this!—I come, I come!   [*Knocking.*
    Who knocks so hard? whence come you? what's your will?

NURSE.   [*Within*] Let me come in, and you shall know my errand;
    I come from Lady Juliet.

FRI. L.   Welcome, then.

Enter NURSE.

NURSE.   O holy Friar, O, tell me, holy Friar,
    Where is my lady's lord, where's Romeo?

FRI. L.   There on the ground, with his own tears made drunk.

NURSE.   O, he is even in my mistress' case,
    Just in her case!

FRI. L.   O woeful sympathy!
    Piteous predicament!

NURSE.   Even so lies she,
    Blubbering and weeping, weeping and blubbering.
    Stand up, stand up; stand, an you be a man:
    For Juliet's sake, for her sake, rise and stand;
    Why should you fall into so deep an O?

ROM.   Nurse!

NURSE.   Ah sir! ah sir! Well, death's the end of all.

ROM.   Spakest thou of Juliet? how is it with her?
    Doth she not think me an old murderer,
    Now I have stain'd the childhood of our joy
    With blood removed but little from her own?
    Where is she? and how doth she? and what says
    My conceal'd lady to our cancell'd love?

NURSE.   O, she says nothing, sir, but weeps and weeps;
    And now falls on her bed; and then starts up,
    And Tybalt calls; and then on Romeo cries,
    And then down falls again.

ROM.   As if that name,

Shot from the deadly level[7] of a gun,
Did murder her, as that name's cursed hand
Murder'd her kinsman. O, tell me, Friar, tell me,
In what vile part of this anatomy
Doth my name lodge? tell me, that I may sack
The hateful mansion.   [*Drawing his sword.*

FRI. L.   Hold thy desperate hand:
Art thou a man? thy form cries out thou art:
Thy tears are womanish; thy wild acts denote
The unreasonable fury of a beast:
Unseemly woman in a seeming man!
Or ill-beseeming beast in seeming both!
Thou hast amazed me: by my holy order,
I thought thy disposition better temper'd.
Hast thou slain Tybalt? wilt thou slay thyself?
And slay thy lady that in thy life lives,
By doing damned hate upon thyself?
Why rail'st thou on thy birth, the heaven and earth?
Since birth and heaven and earth, all three do meet
In thee at once, which thou at once wouldst lose.
Fie, fie, thou shamest thy shape, thy love, thy wit;
Which, like a usurer, abound'st in all,
And usest none in that true use indeed
Which should bedeck thy shape, thy love, thy wit:
Thy noble shape is but a form of wax,
Digressing from the valour of a man;
Thy dear love sworn, but hollow perjury,
Killing that love which thou hast vow'd to cherish;
Thy wit, that ornament to shape and love,
Mis-shapen in the conduct of them both,
Like powder in a skilless soldier's flask,
Is set a-fire by thine own ignorance,
And thou dismember'd with thine own defence.
What, rouse thee, man! thy Juliet is alive,
For whose dear sake thou wast but lately dead;
There art thou happy: Tybalt would kill thee,
But thou slew'st Tybalt; there art thou happy too:
The law, that threaten'd death, becomes thy friend,
And turns it to exile; there art thou happy:

---

[7] *level*] aim.

A pack of blessings lights upon thy back;
Happiness courts thee in her best array;
But, like a misbehaved and sullen wench,
Thou pout'st upon thy fortune and thy love:
Take heed, take heed, for such die miserable.
Go, get thee to thy love, as was decreed,
Ascend her chamber, hence and comfort her:
But look thou stay not till the watch be set,
For then thou canst not pass to Mantua;
Where thou shalt live till we can find a time
To blaze[8] your marriage, reconcile your friends,
Beg pardon of the Prince, and call thee back
With twenty hundred thousand times more joy
Than thou went'st forth in lamentation.
Go before, Nurse: commend me to thy lady,
And bid her hasten all the house to bed,
Which heavy sorrow makes them apt unto:
Romeo is coming.

NURSE.   O Lord, I could have stay'd here all the night
To hear good counsel: O, what learning is!
My lord, I'll tell my lady you will come.

ROM.   Do so, and bid my sweet prepare to chide.

NURSE.   Here, sir, a ring she bid me give you, sir:
Hie you, make haste, for it grows very late.   [*Exit.*

ROM.   How well my comfort is revived by this!

FRI. L.   Go hence; good night; and here stands all your state:
Either be gone before the watch be set,
Or by the break of day disguised from hence:
Sojourn in Mantua; I'll find out your man,
And he shall signify from time to time
Every good hap to you that chances here:
Give me thy hand; 'tis late: farewell; good night.

ROM.   But that a joy past joy calls out on me,
It were a grief, so brief to part with thee:
Farewell.   [*Exeunt.*

---

[8] *blaze*] make public.

SCENE IV. *A room in Capulet's house.*

Enter CAPULET, LADY CAPULET, *and* PARIS.

CAP.   Things have fall'n out, sir, so unluckily,
　　　　That we have had no time to move our daughter.
　　　　Look you, she loved her kinsman Tybalt dearly,
　　　　And so did I. Well, we were born to die.
　　　　'Tis very late; she'll not come down to-night:
　　　　I promise you, but for your company,
　　　　I would have been a-bed an hour ago.
PAR.   These times of woe afford no time to woo.
　　　　Madam, good night: commend me to your daughter.
LA. CAP.   I will, and know her mind early to-morrow;
　　　　To-night she's mew'd up to her heaviness.
CAP.   Sir Paris, I will make a desperate tender[1]
　　　　Of my child's love: I think she will be ruled
　　　　In all respects by me; nay more, I doubt it not.
　　　　Wife, go you to her ere you go to bed;
　　　　Acquaint her here of my son Paris' love;
　　　　And bid her, mark you me, on Wednesday next—
　　　　But, soft! what day is this?
PAR.   　　　　　　　　　　　Monday, my lord.
CAP.   Monday! ha, ha! Well, Wednesday is too soon;
　　　　O' Thursday let it be: o' Thursday, tell her,
　　　　She shall be married to this noble earl.
　　　　Will you be ready? do you like this haste?
　　　　We'll keep no great ado; a friend or two;
　　　　For, hark you, Tybalt being slain so late,
　　　　It may be thought we held him carelessly,
　　　　Being our kinsman, if we revel much:
　　　　Therefore we'll have some half-a-dozen friends,
　　　　And there an end. But what say you to Thursday?
PAR.   My lord, I would that Thursday were to-morrow.
CAP.   Well, get you gone: o' Thursday be it then.
　　　　Go you to Juliet ere you go to bed,

---

[1] *desperate tender*] reckless offer.

Prepare her, wife, against this wedding-day.
Farewell, my lord. Light to my chamber, ho!
Afore me,[2] it is so very very late,
That we may call it early by and by:
Good night.   [*Exeunt.*

SCENE V. *Capulet's orchard.*

Enter ROMEO *and* JULIET, *above, at the window.*

JUL.   Wilt thou be gone? it is not yet near day:
It was the nightingale, and not the lark,
That pierced the fearful hollow of thine ear;
Nightly she sings on yond pomegranate-tree:
Believe me, love, it was the nightingale.

ROM.   It was the lark, the herald of the morn,
No nightingale: look, love, what envious streaks
Do lace the severing clouds in yonder east:
Night's candles are burnt out, and jocund day
Stands tiptoe on the misty mountain tops:
I must be gone and live, or stay and die.

JUL.   Yond light is not day-light, I know it, I:
It is some meteor that the sun exhales,
To be to thee this night a torch-bearer,
And light thee on thy way to Mantua:
Therefore stay yet; thou need'st not to be gone.

ROM.   Let me be ta'en, let me be put to death;
I am content, so thou wilt have it so.
I'll say yon grey is not the morning's eye,
'Tis but the pale reflex of Cynthia's[1] brow;
Nor that is not the lark, whose notes do beat
The vaulty heaven so high above our heads:
I have more care to stay than will to go:
Come, death, and welcome! Juliet wills it so.
How is't, my soul? let's talk: it is not day.

JUL.   It is, it is: hie hence, be gone, away!
It is the lark that sings so out of tune,
Straining harsh discords and unpleasing sharps.

[2] *Afore me*] by my life.

---

[1] *Cynthia's*] the moon's.

Some say the lark makes sweet division;[2]
This doth not so, for she divideth us:
Some say the lark and loathed toad change eyes;
O, now I would they had changed voices too!
Since arm from arm that voice doth us affray,[3]
Hunting thee hence with hunts-up[4] to the day.
O, now be gone; more light and light it grows.

ROM.   More light and light: more dark and dark our woes!

Enter NURSE, *to the chamber.*

NURSE.   Madam!
JUL.   Nurse?
NURSE.   Your lady mother is coming to your chamber:
The day is broke; be wary, look about.   [*Exit.*
JUL.   Then, window, let day in, and let life out.
ROM.   Farewell, farewell! one kiss, and I'll descend.   [*Descends.*
JUL.   Art thou gone so? my lord, my love, my friend!
I must hear from thee every day in the hour,
For in a minute there are many days:
O, by this count I shall be much in years
Ere I again behold my Romeo!
ROM.   Farewell!
I will omit no opportunity
That may convey my greetings, love, to thee.
JUL.   O, think'st thou we shall ever meet again?
ROM.   I doubt it not; and all these woes shall serve
For sweet discourses in our time to come.
JUL.   O God! I have an ill-divining soul.
Methinks I see thee, now thou art below,
As one dead in the bottom of a tomb:
Either my eyesight fails or thou look'st pale.
ROM.   And trust me, love, in my eye so do you:
Dry sorrow drinks our blood. Adieu, adieu!   [*Exit.*
JUL.   O fortune, fortune! all men call thee fickle:
If thou art fickle, what dost thou with him
That is renown'd for faith? Be fickle, fortune;
For then, I hope, thou wilt not keep him long,
But send him back.

---

[2] *division*] melodic variation.
[3] *affray*] frighten.
[4] *hunts-up*] a tune played to awaken huntsmen.

LA. CAP.   [*Within*] Ho, daughter! are you up?
JUL.   Who is't that calls? it is my lady mother!
           Is she not down⁵ so late, or up so early?
           What unaccustom'd cause procures her hither?

Enter LADY CAPULET.

LA. CAP.   Why, how now, Juliet!
JUL.   Madam, I am not well.
LA. CAP.   Evermore weeping for your cousin's death?
           What, wilt thou wash him from his grave with tears?
           An if thou couldst, thou couldst not make him live;
           Therefore have done: some grief shows much of love,
           But much of grief shows still some want of wit.
JUL.   Yet let me weep for such a feeling loss.
LA. CAP.   So shall you feel the loss, but not the friend
           Which you weep for.
JUL.   Feeling so the loss,
           I cannot choose but ever weep the friend.
LA. CAP.   Well, girl, thou weep'st not so much for his death
           As that the villain lives which slaughter'd him.
JUL.   What villain, madam?
LA. CAP.   That same villain, Romeo.
JUL.   [*Aside*] Villain and he be many miles asunder.
           God pardon him! I do, with all my heart;
           And yet no man like he doth grieve my heart.
LA. CAP.   That is because the traitor murderer lives.
JUL.   Ay, madam, from the reach of these my hands:
           Would none but I might venge my cousin's death!
LA. CAP.   We will have vengeance for it, fear thou not:
           Then weep no more. I'll send to one in Mantua,
           Where that same banish'd runagate doth live,
           Shall give him such an unaccustom'd dram
           That he shall soon keep Tybalt company:
           And then, I hope, thou wilt be satisfied.
JUL.   Indeed, I never shall be satisfied
           With Romeo, till I behold him—dead—
           Is my poor heart so for a kinsman vex'd.
           Madam, if you could find out but a man
           To bear a poison, I would temper it,

---

⁵ *down*] in bed.

That Romeo should, upon receipt thereof,
Soon sleep in quiet. O, how my heart abhors
To hear him named, and cannot come to him,
To wreak the love I bore my cousin
Upon his body that hath slaughter'd him!

LA. CAP.   Find thou the means, and I'll find such a man.
But now I'll tell thee joyful tidings, girl.

JUL.   And joy comes well in such a needy time:
What are they, I beseech your ladyship?

LA. CAP.   Well, well, thou hast a careful[6] father, child;
One who, to put thee from thy heaviness,
Hath sorted out a sudden day of joy,
That thou expect'st not, nor I look'd not for.

JUL.   Madam, in happy time, what day is that?

LA. CAP.   Marry, my child, early next Thursday morn,
The gallant, young, and noble gentleman,
The County Paris, at Saint Peter's Church,
Shall happily make thee there a joyful bride.

JUL.   Now, by Saint Peter's Church, and Peter too,
He shall not make me there a joyful bride.
I wonder at this haste; that I must wed
Ere he that should be husband comes to woo.
I pray you, tell my lord and father, madam,
I will not marry yet; and, when I do, I swear,
It shall be Romeo, whom you know I hate,
Rather than Paris. These are news indeed!

LA. CAP.   Here comes your father; tell him so yourself,
And see how he will take it at your hands.

Enter CAPULET *and* NURSE.

CAP.   When the sun sets, the air doth drizzle dew;
But for the sunset of my brother's son
It rains downright.
How now! a conduit,[7] girl? what, still in tears?
Evermore showering? In one little body
Thou counterfeit'st a bark, a sea, a wind:
For still thy eyes, which I may call the sea,
Do ebb and flow with tears; the bark thy body is,

---

[6] *careful*] provident, attentive.
[7] *conduit*] water pipe.

      Sailing in this salt flood; the winds, thy sighs;
      Who raging with thy tears, and they with them,
      Without a sudden calm will overset
      Thy tempest-tossed body. How now, wife!
      Have you deliver'd to her our decree?

LA. CAP.   Ay, sir; but she will none, she gives you thanks.
      I would the fool were married to her grave!

CAP.   Soft! take me with you,[8] take me with you, wife.
      How! will she none? doth she not give us thanks?
      Is she not proud? doth she not count her blest,
      Unworthy as she is, that we have wrought
      So worthy a gentleman to be her bridegroom?

JUL.   Not proud, you have, but thankful that you have:
      Proud can I never be of what I hate;
      But thankful even for hate that is meant love.

CAP.   How, how! how, how! chop-logic! What is this?
      'Proud,' and 'I thank you,' and 'I thank you not';
      And yet 'not proud': mistress minion,[9] you,
      Thank me no thankings, nor proud me no prouds,
      But fettle[10] your fine joints 'gainst Thursday next,
      To go with Paris to Saint Peter's Church,
      Or I will drag thee on a hurdle[11] thither.
      Out, you green-sickness[12] carrion! out, you baggage!
      You tallow-face!

LA. CAP.   Fie, fie! what, are you mad?

JUL.   Good father, I beseech you on my knees,
      Hear me with patience but to speak a word.

CAP.   Hang thee, young baggage! disobedient wretch!
      I tell thee what: get thee to church o' Thursday,
      Or never after look me in the face:
      Speak not, reply not, do not answer me;
      My fingers itch. Wife, we scarce thought us blest
      That God had lent us but this only child;
      But now I see this one is one too much,
      And that we have a curse in having her:

---

[8] *take me with you*] let me understand you.

[9] *minion*] spoiled minx.

[10] *fettle*] prepare.

[11] *hurdle*] a conveyance on which criminals were taken to the place of execution.

[12] *green-sickness*] anemic. Anemia was considered a young woman's ailment. Thus here the implication is "immature," "foolish."

Out on her, hilding!

NURSE.   God in heaven bless her!
     You are to blame, my lord, to rate[13] her so.

CAP.   And why, my lady wisdom? hold your tongue,
     Good prudence; smatter[14] with your gossips, go.

NURSE.   I speak no treason.

CAP.   O, God ye god-den.

NURSE.   May not one speak?

CAP.   Peace, you mumbling fool!
     Utter your gravity[15] o'er a gossip's bowl;
     For here we need it not.

LA. CAP.   You are too hot.

CAP.   God's bread! it makes me mad:
     Day, night, hour, tide, time, work, play,
     Alone, in company, still my care hath been
     To have her match'd: and having now provided
     A gentleman of noble parentage,
     Of fair demesnes, youthful, and nobly train'd,
     Stuff'd, as they say, with honourable parts,
     Proportion'd as one's thought would wish a man;
     And then to have a wretched puling fool,
     A whining mammet,[16] in her fortune's tender,
     To answer 'I'll not wed; I cannot love,
     I am too young; I pray you, pardon me.'
     But, an you will not wed, I'll pardon you:
     Graze where you will, you shall not house with me:
     Look to't, think on't, I do not use to jest.
     Thursday is near; lay hand on heart, advise:
     An you be mine, I'll give you to my friend;
     An you be not, hang, beg, starve, die in the streets,
     For, by my soul, I'll ne'er acknowledge thee,
     Nor what is mine shall never do thee good:
     Trust to't, bethink you; I'll not be forsworn.   [*Exit.*

JUL.   Is there no pity sitting in the clouds,
     That sees into the bottom of my grief?
     O, sweet my mother, cast me not away!
     Delay this marriage for a month, a week;

---

[13] *rate*] berate, scold.
[14] *smatter*] chatter, prattle.
[15] *gravity*] wisdom.
[16] *mammet*] doll, puppet.

Or, if you do not, make the bridal bed
In that dim monument where Tybalt lies.

LA. CAP. Talk not to me, for I'll not speak a word:
Do as thou wilt, for I have done with thee.   [*Exit.*

JUL.   O God!—O Nurse, how shall this be prevented?
My husband is on earth, my faith in heaven;
How shall that faith return again to earth,
Unless that husband send it me from heaven
By leaving earth? comfort me, counsel me.
Alack, alack, that heaven should practise stratagems
Upon so soft a subject as myself!
What say'st thou? hast thou not a word of joy?
Some comfort, Nurse.

NURSE.   Faith, here it is.
Romeo is banish'd, and all the world to nothing,[17]
That he dares ne'er come back to challenge you;
Or, if he do, it needs must be by stealth.
Then, since the case so stands as now it doth,
I think it best you married with the County.
O, he's a lovely gentleman!
Romeo's a dishclout to him: an eagle, madam,
Hath not so green, so quick, so fair an eye
As Paris hath. Beshrew my very heart,
I think you are happy in this second match,
For it excels your first: or if it did not,
Your first is dead, or 'twere as good he were
As living here and you no use of him.

JUL.   Speakest thou from thy heart?

NURSE.   And from my soul too; else beshrew them both.

JUL.   Amen!

NURSE.   What?

JUL.   Well, thou hast comforted me marvellous much.
Go in, and tell my lady I am gone,
Having displeased my father, to Laurence' cell,
To make confession and to be absolved.

NURSE.   Marry, I will, and this is wisely done.   [*Exit.*

JUL.   Ancient damnation![18] O most wicked fiend!
Is it more sin to wish me thus forsworn,

---

[17] *all the world to nothing*] the odds are overwhelmingly against you.
[18] *Ancient damnation*] evil old woman.

Or to dispraise my lord with that same tongue
Which she hath praised him with above compare
So many thousand times? Go, counsellor;
Thou and my bosom henceforth shall be twain.
I'll to the Friar, to know his remedy:
If all else fail, myself have power to die.   [*Exit.*

ACT IV.

SCENE I. *Friar Laurence's cell.*

Enter FRIAR LAURENCE *and* PARIS.

FRI. L.   On Thursday, sir? the time is very short.
PAR.   My father Capulet will have it so;
    And I am nothing slow to slack his haste.
FRI. L.   You say you do not know the lady's mind:
    Uneven is the course; I like it not.
PAR.   Immoderately she weeps for Tybalt's death,
    And therefore have I little talk'd of love,
    For Venus smiles not in a house of tears.
    Now, sir, her father counts it dangerous
    That she doth give her sorrow so much sway,
    And in his wisdom hastes our marriage,
    To stop the inundation of her tears,
    Which, too much minded by herself alone,
    May be put from her by society:
    Now do you know the reason of this haste.
FRI. L.   [*Aside*] I would I knew not why it should be slow'd.
    Look, sir, here comes the lady toward my cell.

Enter JULIET.

PAR.   Happily met, my lady and my wife!
JUL.   That may be, sir, when I may be a wife.
PAR.   That may be must be, love, on Thursday next.
JUL.   What must be shall be.
FRI. L.   That's a certain text.
PAR.   Come you to make confession to this father?

67

JUL. To answer that, I should confess to you.

PAR. Do not deny to him that you love me.

JUL. I will confess to you that I love him.

PAR. So will ye, I am sure, that you love me.

JUL. If I do so, it will be of more price,
      Being spoke behind your back, than to your face.

PAR. Poor soul, thy face is much abused with tears.

JUL. The tears have got small victory by that;
      For it was bad enough before their spite.

PAR. Thou wrong'st it more than tears with that report.

JUL. That is no slander, sir, which is a truth,
      And what I spake, I spake it to my face.

PAR. Thy face is mine, and thou hast slander'd it.

JUL. It may be so, for it is not mine own.
      Are you at leisure, holy father, now;
      Or shall I come to you at evening mass?

FRI. L. My leisure serves me, pensive daughter, now.
      My lord, we must entreat the time alone.

PAR. God shield I should disturb devotion!
      Juliet, on Thursday early will I rouse ye:
      Till then, adieu, and keep this holy kiss.   [*Exit.*

JUL. O, shut the door, and when thou hast done so,
      Come weep with me; past hope, past cure, past help!

FRI. L. Ah, Juliet, I already know thy grief;
      It strains me past the compass of my wits:
      I hear thou must, and nothing may prorogue it,
      On Thursday next be married to this County.

JUL. Tell me not, Friar, that thou hear'st of this,
      Unless thou tell me how I may prevent it:
      If in thy wisdom thou canst give no help,
      Do thou but call my resolution wise,
      And with this knife I'll help it presently.[1]
      God join'd my heart and Romeo's, thou our hands;
      And ere this hand, by thee to Romeo's seal'd,
      Shall be the label to another deed,
      Or my true heart with treacherous revolt
      Turn to another, this shall slay them both:
      Therefore, out of thy long-experienced time,
      Give me some present counsel; or, behold,

----

[1] *presently*] instantly.

'Twixt my extremes[2] and me this bloody knife
Shall play the umpire, arbitrating that
Which the commission of[3] thy years and art
Could to no issue of true honour bring.
Be not so long to speak; I long to die,
If what thou speak'st speak not of remedy.

FRI. L.   Hold, daughter: I do spy a kind of hope,
Which craves as desperate an execution
As that is desperate which we would prevent.
If, rather than to marry County Paris,
Thou hast the strength of will to slay thyself,
Then is it likely thou wilt undertake
A thing like death to chide away this shame,
That copest[4] with death himself to 'scape from it;
And, if thou darest, I'll give thee remedy.

JUL.   O, bid me leap, rather than marry Paris,
From off the battlements of yonder tower;
Or walk in thievish ways; or bid me lurk
Where serpents are; chain me with roaring bears;
Or shut me nightly in a charnel-house,
O'er-cover'd quite with dead men's rattling bones,
With reeky shanks and yellow chapless[5] skulls;
Or bid me go into a new-made grave,
And hide me with a dead man in his shroud;
Things that to hear them told, have made me tremble;
And I will do it without fear or doubt,
To live an unstain'd wife to my sweet love.

FRI. L.   Hold, then; go home, be merry, give consent
To marry Paris: Wednesday is to-morrow;
To-morrow night look that thou lie alone,
Let not thy nurse lie with thee in thy chamber:
Take thou this vial, being then in bed,
And this distilled liquor drink thou off:
When presently through all thy veins shall run
A cold and drowsy humour; for no pulse
Shall keep his native progress, but surcease:
No warmth, no breath, shall testify thou livest;

---

[2] *extremes*] extreme difficulties.
[3] *commission of*] authority deriving from.
[4] *copest*] associates.
[5] *chapless*] without the lower jaw.

The roses in thy lips and cheeks shall fade
To paly ashes; thy eyes' windows fall,
Like death, when he shuts up the day of life;
Each part, deprived of supple government,
Shall, stiff and stark and cold, appear like death:
And in this borrow'd likeness of shrunk death
Thou shalt continue two and forty hours,
And then awake as from a pleasant sleep.
Now, when the bridegroom in the morning comes
To rouse thee from thy bed, there art thou dead:
Then, as the manner of our country is,
In thy best robes uncover'd on the bier
Thou shalt be borne to that same ancient vault
Where all the kindred of the Capulets lie.
In the mean time, against thou shalt awake,
Shall Romeo by my letters know our drift;
And hither shall he come: and he and I
Will watch thy waking, and that very night
Shall Romeo bear thee hence to Mantua.
And this shall free thee from this present shame,
If no inconstant toy[6] nor womanish fear
Abate thy valour in the acting it.

JUL.   Give me, give me! O, tell not me of fear!

FRI. L.   Hold; get you gone, be strong and prosperous
In this resolve: I'll send a friar with speed
To Mantua, with my letters to thy lord.

JUL.   Love give me strength! and strength shall help afford.
Farewell, dear father!   [*Exeunt.*

SCENE II. *Hall in Capulet's house.*

Enter CAPULET, LADY CAPULET, NURSE, *and two* Servingmen.

CAP.   So many guests invite as here are writ.   [*Exit* First Servant.
Sirrah, go hire me twenty cunning cooks.

SEC. SERV.   You shall have none ill, sir, for I'll try if they can lick their
fingers.

CAP.   How canst thou try them so?

---

[6] *toy*] whim, idle fancy.

SEC. SERV.　Marry, sir, 'tis an ill cook that cannot lick his own fingers:
　　　therefore he that cannot lick his fingers goes not with me.
CAP.　Go, be gone.　　　　　　　　　　　　　　　　　[*Exit* Sec. Servant.
　　　We shall be much unfurnish'd[1] for this time.
　　　What, is my daughter gone to Friar Laurence?
NURSE.　Ay, forsooth.
CAP.　Well, he may chance to do some good on her:
　　　A peevish self-will'd harlotry[2] it is.

Enter JULIET.

NURSE.　See where she comes from shrift with merry look.
CAP.　How now, my headstrong! where have you been gadding?
JUL.　Where I have learn'd me to repent the sin
　　　Of disobedient opposition
　　　To you and your behests, and am enjoin'd
　　　By holy Laurence to fall prostrate here,
　　　To beg your pardon: pardon, I beseech you!
　　　Henceforward I am ever ruled by you.
CAP.　Send for the County; go tell him of this:
　　　I'll have this knot knit up to-morrow morning.
JUL.　I met the youthful lord at Laurence' cell,
　　　And gave him what becomed[3] love I might,
　　　Not stepping o'er the bounds of modesty.
CAP.　Why, I am glad on 't; this is well: stand up:
　　　This is as 't should be. Let me see the County;
　　　Ay, marry, go, I say, and fetch him hither.
　　　Now, afore God, this reverend holy Friar,
　　　All our whole city is much bound to him.
JUL.　Nurse, will you go with me into my closet,[4]
　　　To help me sort such needful ornaments
　　　As you think fit to furnish me to-morrow?
LA. CAP.　No, not till Thursday; there is time enough.
CAP.　Go, Nurse, go with her: we'll to church to-morrow.
　　　　　　　　　　　　　　　　[*Exeunt* JULIET *and* NURSE.
LA. CAP.　We shall be short in our provision:
　　　'Tis now near night.
CAP.　　　　　　　　　　　Tush, I will stir about,

---

[1] *unfurnish'd*] unprepared.
[2] *harlotry*] good-for-nothing.
[3] *becomed*] becoming, befitting.
[4] *closet*] private room.

And all things shall be well, I warrant thee, wife:
Go thou to Juliet, help to deck up her;
I'll not to bed to-night; let me alone;
I'll play the housewife for this once. What, ho!
They are all forth: well, I will walk myself
To County Paris, to prepare him up
Against to-morrow: my heart is wondrous light,
Since this same wayward girl is so reclaim'd.   [*Exeunt.*

SCENE III. *Juliet's chamber.*

Enter JULIET *and* NURSE.

JUL.   Ay, those attires are best: but, gentle Nurse,
   I pray thee, leave me to myself to-night;
   For I have need of many orisons
   To move the heavens to smile upon my state,
   Which, well thou know'st, is cross[1] and full of sin.

Enter LADY CAPULET.

LA. CAP.   What, are you busy, ho? need you my help?
JUL.   No, madam; we have cull'd such necessaries
   As are behoveful for our state to-morrow:
   So please you, let me now be left alone,
   And let the Nurse this night sit up with you,
   For I am sure you have your hands full all
   In this so sudden business.
LA. CAP.   Good night:
   Get thee to bed and rest, for thou hast need.
                         [*Exeunt* LADY CAPULET *and* NURSE.
JUL.   Farewell! God knows when we shall meet again.
   I have a faint cold fear thrills through my veins,
   That almost freezes up the heat of life:
   I'll call them back again to comfort me.
   Nurse!—What should she do here?
   My dismal scene I needs must act alone.
   Come, vial.
   What if this mixture do not work at all?

---

[1] *cross*] perverse.

Shall I be married then to-morrow morning?
No, no: this shall forbid it. Lie thou there. [*Laying down a dagger.*
What if it be a poison, which the Friar
Subtly hath minister'd to have me dead,
Lest in this marriage he should be dishonour'd,
Because he married me before to Romeo?
I fear it is: and yet, methinks, it should not,
For he hath still been tried a holy man.
How if, when I am laid into the tomb,
I wake before the time that Romeo
Come to redeem me? there's a fearful point.
Shall I not then be stifled in the vault,
To whose foul mouth no healthsome air breathes in,
And there die strangled ere my Romeo comes?
Or, if I live, is it not very like,
The horrible conceit of death and night,
Together with the terror of the place,
As in a vault, an ancient receptacle,
Where for this many hundred years the bones
Of all my buried ancestors are pack'd;
Where bloody Tybalt, yet but green in earth,
Lies festering in his shroud; where, as they say,
At some hours in the night spirits resort;
Alack, alack, is it not like that I
So early waking, what with loathsome smells
And shrieks like mandrakes' torn out of the earth,
That living mortals hearing them run mad:
O, if I wake, shall I not be distraught,
Environed with all these hideous fears?
And madly play with my forefathers' joints?
And pluck the mangled Tybalt from his shroud?
And, in this rage,[2] with some great kinsman's bone,
As with a club, dash out my desperate brains?
O, look! methinks I see my cousin's ghost
Seeking out Romeo, that did spit his body
Upon a rapier's point: stay, Tybalt, stay!
Romeo, I come! this do I drink to thee.
                    [*She falls upon her bed, within the curtains.*

---

[2] *rage*] madness.

SCENE IV. *Hall in Capulet's house.*

Enter LADY CAPULET *and* NURSE.

LA. CAP.   Hold, take these keys, and fetch more spices, Nurse.
NURSE.   They call for dates and quinces in the pastry.[1]

Enter CAPULET.

CAP.   Come, stir, stir, stir! the second cock hath crow'd,
    The curfew-bell hath rung, 'tis three o'clock:
    Look to the baked meats, good Angelica:
    Spare not for cost.
NURSE.   Go, you cot-quean,[2] go,
    Get you to bed; faith, you'll be sick to-morrow
    For this night's watching.
CAP.   No, not a whit: what! I have watch'd ere now
    All night for lesser cause, and ne'er been sick.
LA. CAP.   Ay, you have been a mouse-hunt[3] in your time;
    But I will watch you from such watching now.
                        [*Exeunt* LADY CAPULET *and* NURSE.
CAP.   A jealous-hood,[4] a jealous-hood!
Enter three or four Servingmen, *with spits, and logs, and baskets.*

                          Now, fellow,
    What's there?
FIRST SERV.   Things for the cook, sir, but I know not what.
CAP.   Make haste, make haste. [*Exit* First Serv.] Sirrah, fetch drier logs:
    Call Peter, he will show thee where they are.
SEC. SERV.   I have a head, sir, that will find out logs,
    And never trouble Peter for the matter.
CAP.   Mass, and well said; a merry whoreson, ha!
    Thou shalt be logger-head.[5] [*Exit* Sec. Serv.] Good faith, 'tis day:
    The County will be here with music straight,

---

[1] *pastry*] room in which pies were made.
[2] *cot-quean*] a man who plays the housewife.
[3] *mouse-hunt*] woman chaser.
[4] *jealous-hood*] jealousy.
[5] *logger-head*] blockhead.

For so he said he would. [*Music within.*] I hear him near.
Nurse! Wife! What, ho! What, Nurse, I say!

Re-enter NURSE.

Go waken Juliet, go and trim her up;
I'll go and chat with Paris: hie, make haste,
Make haste: the bridegroom he is come already:
Make haste, I say.   [*Exeunt.*

SCENE V. *Juliet's chamber.*

Enter NURSE.

NURSE.   Mistress! what, mistress! Juliet! fast,[1] I warrant her, she:
Why, lamb! why, lady! fie, you slug-a-bed!
Why, love, I say! madam! sweet-heart! why, bride!
What, not a word? you take your pennyworths[2] now;
Sleep for a week; for the next night, I warrant,
The County Paris hath set up his rest[3]
That you shall rest but little. God forgive me,
Marry, and amen, how sound is she asleep!
I needs must wake her. Madam, madam, madam!
Ay, let the County take you in your bed;
He'll fright you up, i' faith. Will it not be? [*Undraws the curtains.*
What, dress'd! and in your clothes! and down again!
I must needs wake you. Lady! lady! lady!
Alas, alas! Help, help! my lady's dead!
O, well-a-day, that ever I was born!
Some aqua-vitae, ho! My lord! my lady!

Enter LADY CAPULET.

LA. CAP.   What noise is here?
NURSE.   O lamentable day!
LA. CAP.   What is the matter?
NURSE.   Look, look! O heavy day!
LA. CAP.   O me, O me! My child, my only life,
Revive, look up, or I will die with thee.

---

[1] *fast*] fast asleep.
[2] *pennyworths*] small quantities (of sleep).
[3] *set up his rest*] determined, with a bawdy innuendo of couching the lance for the
charge.

Help, help! call help.

Enter CAPULET.

CAP.   For shame, bring Juliet forth; her lord is come.
NURSE.   She's dead, deceased, she's dead; alack the day!
LA. CAP.   Alack the day, she's dead, she's dead, she's dead!
CAP.   Ha! let me see her. Out, alas! she's cold;
  Her blood is settled and her joints are stiff;
  Life and these lips have long been separated.
  Death lies on her like an untimely frost
  Upon the sweetest flower of all the field.
NURSE.   O lamentable day!
LA. CAP.   O woeful time!
CAP.   Death, that hath ta'en her hence to make me wail,
  Ties up my tongue and will not let me speak.

Enter FRIAR LAURENCE *and* PARIS, *with* Musicians.

FRI. L.   Come, is the bride ready to go to church?
CAP.   Ready to go, but never to return.
  O son, the night before thy wedding-day
  Hath Death lain with thy wife: see, there she lies,
  Flower as she was, deflowered by him.
  Death is my son-in-law, Death is my heir;
  My daughter he hath wedded: I will die,
  And leave him all; life, living, all is Death's.
PAR.   Have I thought long to see this morning's face,
  And doth it give me such a sight as this?
LA. CAP.   Accurst, unhappy, wretched, hateful day!
  Most miserable hour that e'er time saw
  In lasting labour of his pilgrimage!
  But one, poor one, one poor and loving child,
  But one thing to rejoice and solace in,
  And cruel death hath catch'd it from my sight!
NURSE.   O woe! O woeful, woeful, woeful day!
  Most lamentable day, most woeful day,
  That ever, ever, I did yet behold!
  O day! O day! O day! O hateful day!
  Never was seen so black a day as this:
  O woeful day, O woeful day!
PAR.   Beguiled, divorced, wronged, spited, slain!
  Most detestable death, by thee beguiled,

    By cruel cruel thee quite overthrown!
    O love! O life! not life, but love in death!

CAP.   Despised, distressed, hated, martyr'd, kill'd!
    Uncomfortable[4] time, why camest thou now
    To murder, murder our solemnity?[5]
    O child! O child! my soul, and not my child!
    Dead art thou! Alack, my child is dead;
    And with my child my joys are buried!

FRI. L.   Peace, ho, for shame! confusion's[6] cure lives not
    In these confusions. Heaven and yourself
    Had part in this fair maid; now heaven hath all,
    And all the better is it for the maid:
    Your part in her you could not keep from death;
    But heaven keeps his part in eternal life.
    The most you sought was her promotion,
    For 'twas your heaven she should be advanced:
    And weep ye now, seeing she is advanced
    Above the clouds, as high as heaven itself?
    O, in this love, you love your child so ill,
    That you run mad, seeing that she is well:
    She's not well married that lives married long,
    But she's best married that dies married young.
    Dry up your tears, and stick your rosemary
    On this fair corse, and, as the custom is,
    In all her best array bear her to church:
    For though fond nature bids us all lament,
    Yet nature's tears are reason's merriment.

CAP.   All things that we ordained festival,
    Turn from their office to black funeral:
    Our instruments to melancholy bells;
    Our wedding cheer to a sad burial feast;
    Our solemn hymns to sullen dirges change;
    Our bridal flowers serve for a buried corse,
    And all things change them to the contrary.

FRI. L.   Sir, go you in; and, madam, go with him;
    And go, Sir Paris; every one prepare
    To follow this fair corse unto her grave:

---

[4] *Uncomfortable*] joyless.
[5] *solemnity*] celebration, ceremony.
[6] *confusion's*] calamity's.

The heavens do lour upon you for some ill;
Move them no more by crossing their high will.

             [*Exeunt* CAPULET, LADY CAPULET, PARIS, *and* FRIAR.

FIRST MUS.   Faith, we may put up our pipes, and be gone.

NURSE.   Honest good fellows, ah, put up, put up;
    For, well you know, this is a pitiful case.   [*Exit.*

FIRST MUS.   Ay, by my troth, the case may be amended.

Enter PETER.

PET.   Musicians, O, musicians, 'Heart's ease,[7] Heart's ease': O, an you
will have me live, play 'Heart's ease.'

FIRST MUS.   Why 'Heart's ease'?

PET.   O, musicians, because my heart itself plays 'My heart is full of
woe': O, play me some merry dump,[8] to comfort me.

FIRST MUS.   Not a dump we; 'tis no time to play now.

PET.   You will not then?

FIRST MUS.   No.

PET.   I will then give it you soundly.

FIRST MUS.   What will you give us?

PET.   No money, on my faith, but the gleek;[9] I will give you the
minstrel.

FIRST MUS.   Then will I give you the serving-creature.

PET.   Then will I lay the serving-creature's dagger on your pate. I will
carry no crotchets:[10] I'll re you, I'll fa you; do you note me?

FIRST MUS.   An you re us and fa us, you note us.

SEC. MUS.   Pray you, put up your dagger, and put out[11] your wit.

PET.   Then have at you with my wit! I will dry-beat you with an iron
wit, and put up my iron dagger. Answer me like men:

        'When griping grief the heart doth wound
        And doleful dumps the mind oppress,
        Then music with her silver sound'—

why 'silver sound'? why 'music with her silver sound'?—What say
you, Simon Catling?[12]

---

[7] '*Heart's ease*'] a popular tune of the time.
[8] *dump*] melancholy tune.
[9] *gleek*] gesture of scorn.
[10] *carry no crotchets*] endure none of your whims (with the musical pun).
[11] *put out*] display.
[12] *Catling*] a lute string.

FIRST MUS.   Marry, sir, because silver hath a sweet sound.

PET.   Pretty! What say you, Hugh Rebeck?[13]

SEC. MUS.   I say, 'silver sound,' because musicians sound for silver.

PET.   Pretty too! What say you, James Soundpost?

THIRD MUS.   Faith, I know not what to say.

PET.   O, I cry you mercy; you are the singer: I will say for you. It is 'music with her silver sound,' because musicians have no gold for sounding:

> 'Then music with her silver sound
> With speedy help doth lend redress.'   [*Exit.*

FIRST MUS.   What a pestilent knave is this same!

SEC. MUS.   Hang him, Jack! Come, we'll in here; tarry for the mourners, and stay dinner.   [*Exeunt.*

---

[13] *Rebeck*] a three-stringed fiddle.

ACT V.

Scene I. *Mantua. A street.*

Enter ROMEO.

ROM.   If I may trust the flattering truth of sleep,
    My dreams presage some joyful news at hand:
    My bosom's lord sits lightly in his throne,
    And all this day an unaccustom'd spirit
    Lifts me above the ground with cheerful thoughts.
    I dreamt my lady came and found me dead—
    Strange dream, that gives a dead man leave to think!—
    And breathed such life with kisses in my lips,
    That I revived and was an emperor.
    Ah me! how sweet is love itself possess'd,
    When but love's shadows are so rich in joy!

Enter BALTHASAR, *booted.*

    News from Verona! How now, Balthasar!
    Dost thou not bring me letters from the Friar?
    How doth my lady? Is my father well?
    How fares my Juliet? that I ask again;
    For nothing can be ill, if she be well.
BAL.   Then she is well, and nothing can be ill:
    Her body sleeps in Capels' monument,
    And her immortal part with angels lives.
    I saw her laid low in her kindred's vault,
    And presently took post to tell it you:
    O, pardon me for bringing these ill news,
    Since you did leave it for my office, sir.
ROM.   Is it e'en so? then I defy you, stars!

    Thou know'st my lodging: get me ink and paper,
    And hire post-horses; I will hence to-night.
BAL.   I do beseech you, sir, have patience:
    Your looks are pale and wild, and do import
    Some misadventure.
ROM.   Tush, thou art deceived:
    Leave me, and do the thing I bid thee do.
    Hast thou no letters to me from the Friar?
BAL.   No, my good lord.
ROM.   No matter: get thee gone,
    And hire those horses; I'll be with thee straight. [*Exit* BALTHASAR.
    Well, Juliet, I will lie with thee to-night.
    Let's see for means:—O mischief, thou art swift
    To enter in the thoughts of desperate men!
    I do remember an apothecary,
    And hereabouts a' dwells, which late I noted
    In tatter'd weeds, with overwhelming[1] brows,
    Culling of simples;[2] meagre were his looks;
    Sharp misery had worn him to the bones:
    And in his needy shop a tortoise hung,
    An alligator stuff'd and other skins
    Of ill-shaped fishes; and about his shelves
    A beggarly account of empty boxes,
    Green earthen pots, bladders and musty seeds,
    Remnants of packthread and old cakes of roses,[3]
    Were thinly scatter'd, to make up a show.
    Noting this penury, to myself I said,
    An if a man did need a poison now,
    Whose sale is present death in Mantua,
    Here lives a caitiff wretch would sell it him.
    O, this same thought did but forerun my need,
    And this same needy man must sell it me.
    As I remember, this should be the house:
    Being holiday, the beggar's shop is shut.
    What, ho! apothecary!

Enter Apothecary.

---

[1] *overwhelming*] jutting out, overhanging.
[2] *Culling of simples*] gathering medicinal herbs.
[3] *cakes of roses*] rose petals compressed into cakes to be used as perfume.

AP.   Who calls so loud?

ROM.   Come hither, man. I see that thou art poor;
        Hold, there is forty ducats: let me have
        A dram of poison; such soon-speeding gear
        As will disperse itself through all the veins,
        That the life-weary taker may fall dead,
        And that the trunk may be discharged of breath
        As violently as hasty powder fired
        Doth hurry from the fatal cannon's womb.

AP.   Such mortal drugs I have; but Mantua's law
        Is death to any he that utters[+] them.

ROM.   Art thou so bare and full of wretchedness,
        And fear'st to die? famine is in thy cheeks,
        Need and oppression starveth in thy eyes,
        Contempt and beggary hangs upon thy back,
        The world is not thy friend, nor the world's law:
        The world affords no law to make thee rich;
        Then be not poor, but break it, and take this.

AP.   My poverty, but not my will, consents.

ROM.   I pay thy poverty and not thy will.

AP.   Put this in any liquid thing you will,
        And drink it off; and, if you had the strength
        Of twenty men, it would dispatch you straight.

ROM.   There is thy gold, worse poison to men's souls,
        Doing more murder in this loathsome world,
        Than these poor compounds that thou mayst not sell:
        I sell thee poison, thou hast sold me none.
        Farewell: buy food, and get thyself in flesh.
        Come, cordial and not poison, go with me
        To Juliet's grave; for there must I use thee.   [*Exeunt.*

[+] *utters*] dispenses.

SCENE II. *Friar Laurence's cell.*

Enter FRIAR JOHN.

FRI. J.   Holy Franciscan friar! brother, ho!

Enter FRIAR LAURENCE.

FRI. L.   This same should be the voice of Friar John.
     Welcome from Mantua: what says Romeo?
     Or, if his mind be writ, give me his letter.

FRI. J.   Going to find a bare-foot brother out,
     One of our order, to associate[1] me,
     Here in this city visiting the sick,
     And finding him, the searchers of the town,[2]
     Suspecting that we both were in a house
     Where the infectious pestilence did reign,
     Seal'd up the doors and would not let us forth;
     So that my speed to Mantua there was stay'd.

FRI. L.   Who bare my letter then to Romeo?

FRI. J.   I could not send it,—here it is again,—
     Nor get a messenger to bring it thee,
     So fearful were they of infection.

FRI. L.   Unhappy fortune! by my brotherhood,
     The letter was not nice,[3] but full of charge
     Of dear import, and the neglecting it
     May do much danger. Friar John, go hence;
     Get me an iron crow[4] and bring it straight
     Unto my cell.

FRI. J.   Brother, I'll go and bring it thee.   [*Exit.*

FRI. L.   Now must I to the monument alone;
     Within this three hours will fair Juliet wake:
     She will beshrew me much that Romeo
     Hath had no notice of these accidents;
     But I will write again to Mantua,

[1] *associate*] accompany.
[2] *searchers of the town*] officers of the town responsible for public health during a
plague.
[3] *nice*] trivial.
[4] *crow*] crowbar.

And keep her at my cell till Romeo come:
Poor living corse, closed in a dead man's tomb!   [*Exit.*

SCENE III. *A churchyard; in it a monument belonging to the Capulets.*

Enter PARIS *and his* Page, *bearing flowers and a torch.*

PAR.   Give me thy torch, boy: hence, and stand aloof:
        Yet put it out, for I would not be seen.
        Under yond yew-trees lay thee all along,[1]
        Holding thine ear close to the hollow ground;
        So shall no foot upon the churchyard tread,
        Being loose, unfirm, with digging up of graves,
        But thou shalt hear it: whistle then to me,
        As signal that thou hear'st something approach.
        Give me those flowers. Do as I bid thee, go.
PAGE.   [*Aside*] I am almost afraid to stand alone
        Here in the churchyard; yet I will adventure.   [*Retires.*
PAR.   Sweet flower, with flowers thy bridal bed I strew,—
        O woe! thy canopy is dust and stones;—
        Which with sweet water nightly I will dew,
        Or, wanting that, with tears distill'd by moans:
        The obsequies that I for thee will keep
        Nightly shall be to strew thy grave and weep. [*The* Page *whistles.*
        The boy gives warning something doth approach.
        What cursed foot wanders this way to-night,
        To cross my obsequies and true love's rite?
        What, with a torch! Muffle me, night, a while.   [*Retires.*

Enter ROMEO *and* BALTHASAR, *with a torch, mattock, &c.*

ROM.   Give me that mattock and the wrenching iron.
        Hold, take this letter; early in the morning
        See thou deliver it to my lord and father.
        Give me the light: upon thy life, I charge thee,
        Whate'er thou hear'st or seest, stand all aloof,
        And do not interrupt me in my course.
        Why I descend into this bed of death
        Is partly to behold my lady's face,
        But chiefly to take thence from her dead finger

─────────────────────

[1] *all along*] at full length.

A precious ring, a ring that I must use
In dear employment: therefore hence, be gone:
But if thou, jealous,[2] dost return to pry
In what I farther shall intend to do,
By heaven, I will tear thee joint by joint
And strew this hungry churchyard with thy limbs:
The time and my intents are savage-wild,
More fierce and more inexorable far
Than empty tigers or the roaring sea.

BAL.   I will be gone, sir, and not trouble you.

ROM.   So shalt thou show me friendship. Take thou that:
Live, and be prosperous: and farewell, good fellow.

BAL.   *[Aside]* For all this same, I'll hide me hereabout:
His looks I fear, and his intents I doubt.   *[Retires.*

ROM.   Thou detestable maw, thou womb of death,
Gorged with the dearest morsel of the earth,
Thus I enforce thy rotten jaws to open,
And in despite I'll cram thee with more food. *[Opens the tomb.*

PAR.   This is that banish'd haughty Montague
That murder'd my love's cousin, with which grief,
It is supposed, the fair creature died,
And here is come to do some villanous shame
To the dead bodies: I will apprehend him.   *[Comes forward.*
Stop thy unhallow'd toil, vile Montague!
Can vengeance be pursued further than death?
Condemned villain, I do apprehend thee:
Obey, and go with me; for thou must die.

ROM.   I must indeed, and therefore came I hither.
Good gentle youth, tempt not a desperate man;
Fly hence and leave me: think upon these gone;
Let them affright thee. I beseech thee, youth,
Put not another sin upon my head,
By urging me to fury: O, be gone!
By heaven, I love thee better than myself,
For I come hither arm'd against myself:
Stay not, be gone: live, and hereafter say,
A madman's mercy bid thee run away.

PAR.   I do defy thy conjurations[3]
And apprehend thee for a felon here.

---

[2] *jealous*] suspicious.
[3] *conjurations*] solemn appeals.

Rom.   Wilt thou provoke me? then have at thee, boy!   [*They fight.*
Page.   O Lord, they fight! I will go call the watch.   [*Exit.*
Par.   O, I am slain! [*Falls.*] If thou be merciful,
             Open the tomb, lay me with Juliet.   [*Dies.*
Rom.   In faith, I will. Let me peruse this face:
             Mercutio's kinsman, noble County Paris!
             What said my man, when my betossed soul
             Did not attend him as we rode? I think
             He told me Paris should have married Juliet:
             Said he not so? or did I dream it so?
             Or am I mad, hearing him talk of Juliet,
             To think it was so? O, give me thy hand,
             One writ with me in sour misfortune's book!
             I'll bury thee in a triumphant grave;
             A grave? O, no, a lantern,[4] slaughter'd youth;
             For here lies Juliet, and her beauty makes
             This vault a feasting presence[5] full of light.
             Death, lie thou there, by a dead man interr'd.
                                   [*Laying* Paris *in the monument.*
             How oft when men are at the point of death
             Have they been merry! which their keepers call
             A lightning before death: O, how may I
             Call this a lightning? O my love! my wife!
             Death, that hath suck'd the honey of thy breath,
             Hath had no power yet upon thy beauty:
             Thou art not conquer'd; beauty's ensign yet
             Is crimson in thy lips and in thy cheeks,
             And death's pale flag is not advanced there.
             Tybalt, liest thou there in thy bloody sheet?
             O, what more favour can I do to thee
             Than with that hand that cut thy youth in twain
             To sunder his that was thine enemy?
             Forgive me, cousin! Ah, dear Juliet,
             Why art thou yet so fair? shall I believe
             That unsubstantial death is amorous,
             And that the lean abhorred monster keeps
             Thee here in dark to be his paramour?
             For fear of that, I still will stay with thee,

[4] *lantern*] turret full of windows.
[5] *presence*] presence chamber.

And never from this palace of dim night
Depart again: here, here will I remain
With worms that are thy chamber-maids; O, here
Will I set up my everlasting rest,
And shake the yoke of inauspicious stars
From this world-wearied flesh. Eyes, look your last!
Arms, take your last embrace! and, lips, O you
The doors of breath, seal with a righteous kiss
A dateless[6] bargain to engrossing death!
Come, bitter conduct, come, unsavoury guide!
Thou desperate pilot, now at once run on
The dashing rocks thy sea-sick weary bark.
Here's to my love! [*Drinks.*] O true apothecary!
Thy drugs are quick. Thus with a kiss I die.   [*Dies.*

Enter, at the other end of the churchyard, FRIAR LAURENCE, *with a
lantern, crow, and spade.*

FRI. L.   Saint Francis be my speed![7] how oft to-night
           Have my old feet stumbled at graves! Who's there?
BAL.   Here's one, a friend, and one that knows you well.
FRI. L.   Bliss be upon you! Tell me, good my friend,
           What torch is yond that vainly lends his light
           To grubs and eyeless skulls? as I discern,
           It burneth in the Capels' monument.
BAL.   It doth so, holy sir; and there's my master,
           One that you love.
FRI. L.   Who is it?
BAL.   Romeo.
FRI. L.   How long hath he been there?
BAL.   Full half an hour.
FRI. L.   Go with me to the vault.
BAL.   I dare not, sir:
           My master knows not but I am gone hence;
           And fearfully did menace me with death,
           If I did stay to look on his intents.
FRI. L.   Stay, then; I'll go alone: fear comes upon me;
           O, much I fear some ill unlucky thing.
BAL.   As I did sleep under this yew-tree here,

---

[6] *dateless*] eternal.

[7] *speed*] protecting and assisting power.

I dreamt my master and another fought,
And that my master slew him.
FRI. L.   Romeo!   [*Advances.*
   Alack, alack, what blood is this, which stains
   The stony entrance of this sepulchre?
   What mean these masterless and gory swords
   To lie discolour'd by this place of peace?   [*Enters the tomb.*
   Romeo! O, pale! Who else? what, Paris too?
   And steep'd in blood? Ah, what an unkind hour
   Is guilty of this lamentable chance!
   The lady stirs.   [JULIET *wakes.*
JUL.   O comfortable Friar! where is my lord?
   I do remember well where I should be,
   And there I am: where is my Romeo?   [*Noise within.*
FRI. L.   I hear some noise. Lady, come from that nest
   Of death, contagion and unnatural sleep:
   A greater power than we can contradict
   Hath thwarted our intents: come, come away:
   Thy husband in thy bosom there lies dead;
   And Paris too: come, I'll dispose of thee
   Among a sisterhood of holy nuns:
   Stay not to question, for the watch is coming;
   Come, go, good Juliet; I dare no longer stay.
JUL.   Go, get thee hence, for I will not away.   [*Exit* FRI. L.
   What's here? a cup, closed in my true love's hand?
   Poison, I see, hath been his timeless end:
   O churl! drunk all, and left no friendly drop
   To help me after? I will kiss thy lips;
   Haply some poison yet doth hang on them,
   To make me die with a restorative.   [*Kisses him.*
   Thy lips are warm.
FIRST WATCH.   [*Within*] Lead, boy: which way?
JUL.   Yea, noise? then I'll be brief. O happy dagger!
                      [*Snatching* ROMEO'S *dagger.*
   This is thy sheath [*Stabs herself*]; there rust, and let me die.
              [*Falls on* ROMEO'S *body, and dies.*

Enter Watch, *with the* Page *of* PARIS.

PAGE.   This is the place; there, where the torch doth burn.
FIRST WATCH.   The ground is bloody; search about the churchyard:

Go, some of you, whoe'er you find attach.[8]
Pitiful sight! here lies the County slain;
And Juliet bleeding, warm, and newly dead,
Who here hath lain this two days buried.
Go, tell the Prince: run to the Capulets:
Raise up the Montagues: some others search:
We see the ground whereon these woes do lie;
But the true ground of all these piteous woes
We cannot without circumstance[9] descry.

Re-enter some of the Watch, *with* BALTHASAR.

SEC. WATCH.   Here's Romeo's man; we found him in the churchyard.
FIRST WATCH.   Hold him in safety, till the Prince come hither.

Re-enter FRIAR LAURENCE, *and another* Watchman.

THIRD WATCH.   Here is a friar, that trembles, sighs and weeps:
We took this mattock and this spade from him,
As he was coming from this churchyard's side.
FIRST WATCH.   A great suspicion: stay the friar too.

Enter the PRINCE *and* Attendants.

PRINCE.   What misadventure is so early up,
That calls our person from our morning rest?

Enter CAPULET, LADY CAPULET, *and others.*

CAP.   What should it be that they so shriek abroad?
LA. CAP.   The people in the street cry Romeo,
Some Juliet, and some Paris, and all run
With open outcry toward our monument.
PRINCE.   What fear is this which startles in our ears?
FIRST WATCH.   Sovereign, here lies the County Paris slain;
And Romeo dead; and Juliet, dead before,
Warm and new kill'd.
PRINCE.   Search, seek, and know how this foul murder comes.
FIRST WATCH.   Here is a friar, and slaughter'd Romeo's man,
With instruments upon them fit to open
These dead men's tombs.
CAP.   O heavens! O wife, look how our daughter bleeds!

---

[8] *attach*] arrest.
[9] *circumstance*] detailed information.

This dagger hath mista'en, for, lo, his house
Is empty on the back of Montague,
And it mis-sheathed in my daughter's bosom!

LA. CAP.   O me! this sight of death is as a bell
That warns my old age to a sepulchre.

Enter MONTAGUE *and others.*

PRINCE.   Come, Montague; for thou art early up,
To see thy son and heir more early down.

MON.   Alas, my liege, my wife is dead to-night;
Grief of my son's exile hath stopp'd her breath:
What further woe conspires against mine age?

PRINCE.   Look, and thou shalt see.

MON.   O thou untaught! what manners is in this,
To press before thy father to a grave?

PRINCE.   Seal up the mouth of outrage[10] for a while,
Till we can clear these ambiguities,
And know their spring, their head, their true descent;
And then will I be general of your woes,
And lead you even to death: meantime forbear,
And let mischance be slave to patience.
Bring forth the parties of suspicion.

FRI. L.   I am the greatest, able to do least,
Yet most suspected, as the time and place
Doth make against me, of this direful murder;
And here I stand, both to impeach and purge
Myself condemned and myself excused.

PRINCE.   Then say at once what thou dost know in this.

FRI. L.   I will be brief, for my short date of breath
Is not so long as is a tedious tale.
Romeo, there dead, was husband to that Juliet;
And she, there dead, that Romeo's faithful wife:
I married them; and their stol'n marriage-day
Was Tybalt's dooms-day, whose untimely death
Banish'd the new-made bridegroom from this city;
For whom, and not for Tybalt, Juliet pined.
You, to remove that siege of grief from her,
Betroth'd and would have married her perforce
To County Paris: then comes she to me,

---

[10] *outrage*] outcry.

And with wild looks bid me devise some mean
To rid her from this second marriage,
Or in my cell there would she kill herself.
Then gave I her, so tutor'd by my art,
A sleeping potion; which so took effect
As I intended, for it wrought on her
The form of death: meantime I writ to Romeo,
That he should hither come as this dire night,
To help to take her from her borrow'd grave,
Being the time the potion's force should cease.
But he which bore my letter, Friar John,
Was stay'd by accident, and yesternight
Return'd my letter back. Then all alone
At the prefixed hour of her waking
Came I to take her from her kindred's vault,
Meaning to keep her closely[11] at my cell
Till I conveniently could send to Romeo:
But when I came, some minute ere the time
Of her awaking, here untimely lay
The noble Paris and true Romeo dead.
She wakes, and I entreated her come forth,
And bear this work of heaven with patience:
But then a noise did scare me from the tomb,
And she too desperate would not go with me,
But, as it seems, did violence on herself.
All this I know; and to the marriage
Her nurse is privy: and, if aught in this
Miscarried by my fault, let my old life
Be sacrificed some hour before his time
Unto the rigour of severest law.

PRINCE.   We still[12] have known thee for a holy man.
Where's Romeo's man? what can he say in this?

BAL.   I brought my master news of Juliet's death,
And then in post he came from Mantua
To this same place, to this same monument.
This letter he early bid me give his father,
And threaten'd me with death, going in the vault,
If I departed not and left him there.

---

[11] *closely*] in secret.
[12] *still*] always.

PRINCE.   Give me the letter; I will look on it.
      Where is the County's page, that raised the watch?
      Sirrah, what made your master in this place?
PAGE.   He came with flowers to strew his lady's grave;
      And bid me stand aloof, and so I did:
      Anon comes one with light to ope the tomb;
      And by and by my master drew on him;
      And then I ran away to call the watch.
PRINCE.   This letter doth make good the Friar's words,
      Their course of love, the tidings of her death:
      And here he writes that he did buy a poison
      Of a poor 'pothecary, and therewithal
      Came to this vault to die and lie with Juliet.
      Where be these enemies? Capulet! Montague!
      See, what a scourge is laid upon your hate,
      That heaven finds means to kill your joys with love!
      And I, for winking at your discords too,
      Have lost a brace of kinsmen: all are punish'd.
CAP.   O brother Montague, give me thy hand:
      This is my daughter's jointure,[13] for no more
      Can I demand.
MON.   But I can give thee more:
      For I will raise her statue in pure gold;
      That whiles Verona by that name is known,
      There shall no figure at such rate[14] be set
      As that of true and faithful Juliet.
CAP.   As rich shall Romeo's by his lady's lie;
      Poor sacrifices of our enmity!
PRINCE.   A glooming peace this morning with it brings;
      The sun for sorrow will not show his head:
      Go hence, to have more talk of these sad things;
      Some shall be pardon'd and some punished:
      For never was a story of more woe
      Than this of Juliet and her Romeo.   [*Exeunt.*

---

[13] *jointure*] the marriage portion supplied by the bridegroom.
[14] *rate*] value.

Study Guide

Text by
Judy Clamon
(M.A., East Texas State University)

Department of English
Mabank High School
Mabank, Texas

Contents

> **Each scene includes List of Characters,**
> **Summary, Analysis, Study Questions and**
> **Answers, and Suggested Essay Topics.**

SECTION ONE

Introduction

The Life and Work of William Shakespeare

Details about William Shakespeare's life are sketchy, mostly mere surmise based upon court or other clerical records. His parents, John and Mary (Arden), were married about 1557; she was of the landed gentry, and he a yeoman—a glover and commodities merchant. By 1568, John had risen through the ranks of town government and held the position of high bailiff, similar to mayor. William, the eldest son and the third of eight children, was born in 1564, probably on April 23, several days before his baptism on April 26 in Stratford-upon-Avon. Shakespeare is also believed to have died on the same date—April 23—in 1616.

It is believed William attended the local grammar school in Stratford where his parents lived, and studied primarily Latin rhetoric, logic, and literature. At age 18 (1582), William married Anne Hathaway, a local farmer's daughter who was eight years his senior. Their first daughter (Susanna) was born six months later (1583), and twins Judith and Hamnet were born in 1585.

Shakespeare's life can be divided into three periods: the first 20 years in Stratford, which include his schooling, early marriage, and fatherhood; the next 25 years as an actor and playwright in London; and the last five in retirement back in Stratford where he enjoyed moderate wealth gained from his theatrical successes. The years linking the first two periods are marked by a lack of information about Shakespeare, and are often referred to as the "dark years."

Shakespeare probably left school at age 15, which was the norm, to take a job, especially since this was the period of his father's financial difficulty. Numerous references in his plays suggest that William may have in fact worked for his father, in addition to a myriad of other jobs, thereby gaining specialized knowledge.

At some point during the "dark years," Shakespeare began his career with a London theatrical company, perhaps in 1589, for he was already an actor and playwright of some note by 1592.

Shakespeare apparently wrote and acted for numerous theatrical companies, including Pembroke's Men, and Strange's Men, which later became the Chamberlain's Men, with whom he remained for the rest of his career.

In 1592, the Plague closed the theaters for about two years, and Shakespeare turned to writing book length narrative poetry. Most notable were "Venus and Adonis" and "The Rape of Lucrece," both of which were dedicated to the Earl of Southampton, whom scholars accept as Shakespeare's friend and benefactor despite a lack of documentation. During this same period, Shakespeare was writing his sonnets, which are more likely signs of the time's fashion rather than actual love poems detailing any particular relationship. He returned to playwriting when theaters reopened in 1594, and did not continue to write poetry. His sonnets were published without his consent in 1609, shortly before his retirement.

Amid all of his success, Shakespeare suffered the loss of his only son, Hamnet, who died in 1596 at the age of 11.

But Shakespeare's career continued unabated; and in London in 1599, he became one of the partners in the new Globe Theater, which was built by the Chamberlain's Men.

When Queen Elizabeth died in 1603 and was succeeded by her cousin King James of Scotland, the Chamberlain's Men was renamed the King's Men. Shakespeare's productivity and popularity continued uninterrupted. He invested in London real estate and, one year away from retirement, purchased a second theater, the Blackfriars Gatehouse, in partnership with his fellow actors.

Shakespeare wrote very little after 1612, which was the year he completed *Henry VIII*. It was during a performance of this play in 1613 that the Globe caught fire and burned to the ground. Sometime between 1610 and 1613, Shakespeare returned to Stratford, where he owned a large house and property, to spend his remaining years with his family.

William Shakespeare died on April 23, 1616, and was buried two days later in the chancel of Holy Trinity Church where he had been baptized exactly 52 years earlier. His literary legacy included 37 plays, 154 sonnets and five major poems. .

Incredibly, most of Shakespeare's plays had never been published in anything except pamphlet form, and were simply extant as acting scripts stored at the Globe. Theater scripts were not regarded as literary works of art, but only the basis for the performance. Plays were simply a popular form of entertainment for all layers of society in Shakespeare's time. Only the efforts of two of Shakespeare's company, John Heminges and Henry Condell, preserved his 36 plays (minus *Pericles*, the thirty-seventh).

Historical Background

The first permanent professional theater in England was built around 1576 and was called the Theater. Other theaters soon opened, including two called the Curtain and the Rose. Not only was Shakespeare working as a playwright and an actor for the Theater, he was also a stock holder.

Another theater soon opened and became one of the most famous of the London public playhouses. It was completed around 1599 and was called the Globe. It was perhaps the largest theater in England and derived its name "from the sign painted above its door, a picture of Atlas holding the world on his shoulders" (Kittredge). Shakespeare also owned stock in the Globe and performed as an actor in many of his own plays. The Globe was an enclosed theater without a roof. The spectators who stood or sat on the ground around the acting area were called "groundlings." The wealthier playgoers sat in galleries surrounding the stage area. There was no curtain, and sunlight provided the lighting for the performances; therefore, the performances were held during the day. Because there were no sets or scene changes, Shakespeare's characters wore extravagant costumes to provide the beauty and pageantry that was expected on the stage. Plays were usually fast-paced and colorful productions. The actors, as a rule, played more than one part in a play, and all of the women's parts were portrayed by young boys.

Shakespeare began writing comedies from about 1594 to 1603. During this period he produced such works as *The Taming of the Shrew, Two Gentlemen of Verona, A Midsummer-Night's Dream, The Merchant of Venice, Much Ado About Nothing,* and *Twelfth Night.* Two of Shakespeare's tragedies were also written during this time period. One was *Julius Caesar* and the other was *Romeo and Juliet.*

The play version of *Romeo and Juliet* was probably written early in his career around 1595 to 1596. The play is considered to be a tragedy and portrays the interplay of human character and motive. Much of *Romeo and Juliet* is written in blank verse, which is unrhymed iambic pentameter. Iambic simply means a metrical foot made up of an unstressed and stressed syllable, and pentameter means that each line has five metrical feet. While most of *Romeo and Juliet* is written in iambic pentameter, the characters of lower social position speak in prose.

The play is rich in rhyming words, word plays, and puns. Most of Shakespeare's plays begin with a great deal of action designed to capture the attention of the groundlings immediately. Therefore, *Romeo and Juliet* begins with a street fight between the servants of the Capulets and the Montagues, the warring families in the play.

The plot of *Romeo and Juliet* was taken from an earlier version of the story. The theme appeared in the fourth century in a Greek tale and later in the sixteenth century as Luigi da Porto's *Hystoria di due nobili Amanti.* In the later version, the city is Verona, and da Porto was the first to call the hero and heroine Romeo and Giulietta. Probably Shakespeare's most direct source was a long English narrative poem written in 1562 by Arthur Brooke, called *The Tragicall Historye of Romeus and Juliet.* Shakespeare used the characters in Brooke's poem but developed them in much greater depth and detail, thus transforming the story of star-crossed lovers into the most famous love story ever known.

Master List of Characters

Friends and Relatives of the Montague Family:

Romeo—*Son of Montague who falls in love with Juliet*

Montague—*Head of the family who is at war with the Capulets and father to Romeo*

Lady Montague—*Wife to Lord Montague and mother to Romeo*

Mercutio—*A kinsman to the prince and a friend to Romeo*

Benvolio—*A gentle and peace-loving young man who is nephew to Montague and a friend to Romeo*

Balthasar—*A loyal friend and servant to Romeo*

Abram—*A servant of the Montague family*

Friends and Relatives of the Capulet Family:

Juliet—*Daughter of Capulet who falls in love with Romeo*

Tybalt—*A fiery tempered young man who is the nephew of Lady Capulet and cousin to Juliet*

Capulet—*Head of the family who is at war with the Montagues and father to Juliet*

Lady Capulet—*Wife to Lord Capulet and mother to Juliet*

Nurse—*A witty nurse and friend to Juliet*

Sampson—*A servant of the Capulet family*

Gregory—*A servant of the Capulet family*

Peter—*A servant to Juliet's nurse*

Other Characters:

Chorus—*Introduces the play, and sets scene in Acts I and II*

Paris—*Kinsman to the prince and a young nobleman who asks for Juliet's hand in marriage*

Escalus—*The prince of Verona*

Friar Laurence—*A Franciscan friar who marries the lovers in hopes of making peace with the two warring families*

Friar John—*A Franciscan friar who was entrusted with an important letter to Romeo*

Apothecary—*A poor druggist in Mantua who sells poison to Romeo*

Page—*A servant to Paris*

Summary of the Play

The play opens with the servants of the Montague and Capulet families quarreling and fighting in the streets of Verona, Italy. The two families have been enemies for as long as anyone can remember. Romeo, son of Lord Montague, accidentally finds out about a ball given by Lord Capulet and plans to attend uninvited. Romeo and his friends Mercutio and Benvolio put on masks and attend the ball, where Romeo meets the beautiful Juliet and falls instantly in love. Later that night Romeo goes to Juliet's balcony and they exchange vows of love. Romeo enlists the help of Friar Laurence, who agrees to marry the young lovers in hopes of ending the long-standing feud between the two families.

Romeo returns from his wedding and finds that his friend Mercutio is engaged in combat with Tybalt, a member of the Capulet family. Tybalt kills Mercutio. Romeo, enraged over his friend's death, then slays Tybalt. Romeo immediately realizes that he has murdered his wife's cousin and flees to Friar Laurence for help. He also learns that the Prince has banned him from the city under penalty of death if he is found within its borders. Friar Laurence arranges for Romeo to spend one last night with Juliet before he flees to Mantua.

In the meantime, Lord Capulet, unaware that Juliet is married to Romeo, has promised her hand in marriage to Paris. When Juliet is told of the arranged marriage, she is desperate and seeks the help of Friar Laurence, who gives her a vial of sleeping potion. The potion will have a death-like but temporary effect. The plan is for Juliet to take the potion, appear to be dead, and be laid out in the family vault. Romeo will come to the vault the next night, and be there waiting when she awakens. The couple will then flee to Mantua to live. Friar Laurence sends the important message to Romeo telling him of his plan to help Juliet, but the message never reaches Romeo. Juliet, assured by Friar Laurence that Romeo will be waiting for her when she awakens in the tomb, goes home and drinks the potion.

Hearing that Juliet is dead, Romeo purchases poison from a poor apothecary and rushes to her tomb. Upon his arrival, he finds Paris, also in mourning. Thinking that Romeo has come to rob the tomb, Paris fights with Romeo. Romeo kills Paris, enters into the tomb, and buries Paris there. He then bids farewell to Juliet and takes the poison. Awakening from her death-like sleep, Juliet discovers her dead lover and kills herself with Romeo's dagger. Friar Laurence arrives too late to save the lovers and tells the Prince the entire story. The Montagues and Capulets promise to end their hostilities, which have caused the deaths of their only children.

Estimated Reading Time

Because of the play form and the language of Shakespeare, an average student should spend about an hour per act in individual reading. Each act may be broken down into two or three scenes at a time to ensure understanding. The language might be difficult at first, and will require careful examination of footnotes or helps located in the text. After reading each scene, you should answer all study questions in relation to that scene to ensure understanding and comprehension. The essay questions may be used if needed. Since there are five acts in *Romeo and Juliet*, you should expect to spend approximately five hours divided in segments of eight to ten sessions.

SECTION TWO

Act I

Act I, Scenes I and II (pages 2–11)

New Characters:

Chorus

Sampson: *a servant in the Capulet household*

Gregory: *a servant in the Capulet household*

Benvolio: *a peace-loving friend to Romeo and the Montague family*

Tybalt: *a fiery-tempered member of the Capulet family*

Lord Capulet: *the head of the Capulet household*

Lady Capulet: *the wife of Lord Capulet and mother of Juliet*

Lord Montague: *the head of the Montague household*

Lady Montague: *the wife of Lord Montague and the mother of Romeo*

Prince Escalus: *the Prince of Verona whose job is to keep the peace*

Romeo: *the tragic hero of the play who falls in love with the enemy's daughter, Juliet*

Paris: *the young nobleman who is asking Lord Capulet for Juliet's hand in marriage*

Servant: *a servant to the Capulet family who has been asked to deliver invitations to the ball*

Abram: *servant to Montague*

Summary

Before the action of Act I begins, the Chorus sets the stage with the Prologue, which summarizes the basic plot of the play. It states that two families in Verona have been bitter enemies for centuries. The fighting has broken out again between the families. A child from each of the warring families meet and fall in love, and it is the death of the children that finally ends the feud between the parents.

Scene I opens in Verona, Italy, with two Capulet servants walking down the street hoping to meet and start a fight with servants from the Montague family. Sampson decides to start the fight by biting his thumb at the Montague servants. This is an insulting gesture and sure to help start a quarrel. Gregory tells Sampson that he will back him up. They meet the Montague servants and a fight ensues. As the fighting progresses, even the townspeople take sides and become involved, resulting in a street brawl.

Benvolio enters and attempts to break up the fighting, but Tybalt also comes on the scene and challenges him to a duel. Just as Lord Capulet and Lord Montague call for their swords in order to enter into the fight, the Prince and his attendants arrive and break up the quarrel. The Prince threatens to execute anyone who breaks the peace with another brawl in Verona. He requests that Lord Capulet meet him privately and tells Lord Montague that he will talk with him that afternoon.

Benvolio relates the circumstances of the fight to Lord Montague. Lady Montague asks where Romeo is, and Benvolio tells her that he saw him out walking at dawn. Lord Montague is worried about Romeo and states that something is bothering him; however, no one can find out what it is. It seems that he has been seen walking in the night and at dawn with tears in his eyes; but, when the sun comes up, he retreats into his room and pulls the curtains against all light. Romeo approaches, and Benvolio promises to find out what is bothering him.

Benvolio meets Romeo and asks him what "sadness lengthens his (Romeo's) hours." Romeo replies that not having the love that he wants has made him unhappy. It seems that the woman he loves (Rosaline) has sworn not to fall in love. Benvolio encourages Romeo to forget her by comparing her beauty with that of other girls in Verona. Romeo replies that a comparison with other girls would only make her appear even more beautiful. Benvolio states that he will get him to forget her or die trying.

Scene II also takes place on a street in Verona. Lord Capulet is discussing the recent brawl with Paris, a young nobleman. Capulet states that as old as he and Lord Montague are, it will not be too difficult to keep the peace.

Paris has asked for Juliet's hand in marriage and is asking for a reply from Lord Capulet. Lord Capulet tells Paris that he feels that thirteen is too young, but allows Paris to try to sway her into accepting his offer. If Juliet consents, Lord Capulet will also.

Lord Capulet tells Paris that he is giving an "old accustomed feast" this night and invites him to attend. Lord Capulet then hands an invitation list to a servant to deliver throughout the city, not realizing that the servant cannot read.

The servant is disgruntled because he cannot read the list and states that people should stick with what they know best. At that moment, Romeo and Benvolio enter, and the servant asks Romeo if he can read the list to him. Romeo reads the invitation list, and the servant invites him to attend the feast if he is not from the house of Montague. Romeo asks where the feast is to be held, and the servant replies that it is to be held at his master's house, the house of the "great rich Capulet."

Benvolio hears the name of Rosaline (the woman with whom Romeo thinks he is in love) on the list and persuades Romeo to attend the feast in order to compare the beauty of Rosaline with all the other beauties in Verona. Romeo agrees to go, but only to stand and stare at Rosaline.

Analysis

Before the action in Act I begins, Shakespeare uses a chorus to sum up or preview the plot of the play for the audience. The Chorus presents the Prologue of the play as a sonnet, and it serves three distinct purposes. First, it serves to introduce an atmosphere of conflict between two families which paradoxically yokes together the themes of love and violence. Second, it directs the reader's attention to the important part fate plays in the lives of the lovers. Third, it points out that the fate of the lovers is not within their control.

The paradoxical theme of love and death, as announced in the Prologue, indicates the fate of the lovers with such words as "star-crossed," "fatal loins," and "death-marked love." The Prologue also establishes that the lovers are victims of both their parents' hate and an aggressive, violent society that regenerates itself with the breeding of more hate. The Prologue sums up the setting, the plot, the play's ending, the role of fate in the play's development, and the length of time the play will take on the Elizabethan stage.

The plot of *Romeo and Juliet* only encompasses five days in the lives of the characters, and it is important to follow closely the day on which each event occurs. Scenes I and II take place on the first day, and it is a Sunday at nine in the morning.

In Scene I, the action of the play begins on the streets of Verona with the servants of the feuding families instigating a fight. The feud between the families is an ancient, bitter hatred that has affected the entire city and become a public issue. Even the towns-people of Verona have become involved in the fight. Shakespeare intended to begin his play with a street fight in order to appeal to the common people and immediately gain the attention of the groundlings who might become restless quickly.

The quarrel between the servants is an opportunity for Shakespeare to introduce the feud humorously. The Capulet servants banter as they swagger down Verona's streets. The play on words (choler-collar) delighted the Elizabethan audience. Shakespeare relieves the tension brought about by the fiery-tempered Tybalt through his use of humor. When Lord Capulet requests his long sword, his wife retorts, "A crutch, a crutch! Why call you for a sword?" She insinuates that because of his age, a crutch might be more appropriate.

Foreshadowing should be noted in the Prince's speech to the warring families. He states that brawling has broken out three times. Each fight has disturbed the "quiet of our streets" and caused the citizens of Verona to begin fighting again. The Prince's warning words are, "If ever you disturb our streets again, your lives shall pay the forfeit of the peace." He decrees that the punishment for future fighting will be death. The Prince is the voice of authority in Verona. His rule is absolute, and the consequences of his warning will surface in future scenes as the plot progresses.

The theme of love coexisting with hate or death is echoed in Shakespeare's word play and is vividly seen in the form of oxymorons in the following passage: "O brawling love! O loving hate!...O heavy lightness! serious vanity! / Mis-shapen chaos of well-seeming forms! / Feather of lead, bright smoke, cold fire, sick health! / Still-waking sleep...." The concepts of love and death or hate do not naturally go together, but represent opposites. Romeo uses these images to describe love. His selection of words also echo the strife of civil violence.

Since tragedy emphasizes character over fate, the characters become responsible for their own destruction. However, it is fate that manipulates the characters' decisions and development. Fate leads them into the circumstances that will ultimately help destroy them. Therefore, fate plays a tremendous part in the plot of *Romeo and Juliet*. Chance, coincidence, circumstance, and change are all dramatic means by which fate is given its influence in the play. The connection of character with the deed and the catastrophe sets the course of the tragedy, and its outcome is inevitable. The role of chance should be noted in such events as Lord Capulet giving the invitation list to a servant who cannot read, the servant asking Romeo to read the list of names and then inviting him to the feast, and Rosaline's appears on the invitation list. Benvolio then convinces Romeo to attend the ball in order to compare her beauty with the other girls who will be attending.

Romeo's character develops as he moves from a shallow infatuation for Rosaline to a mature romantic love for Juliet later in the play. In Act I, Romeo is portrayed as moody and melancholy. His "love" for Rosaline is not returned by her, and it has become a tormenting sickness to him. Benvolio asks, "What sadness lengthens Romeo's hours?" Romeo responds by saying, "Not having that which having makes them short." His unhappiness illustrates the emptiness of his love. Romeo, in Scene II, is suffering and listless in his love for Rosaline. Benvolio makes a universal observation when he states, "Alas that love, so gentle in his view, should be so tyrannous and rough in proof." Benvolio points out that love is gentle in appearance but mean and rough in reality.

Love is illustrated in two different ways during the play. Not only is there a comparison of youthful, shallow love to the more mature love shared by Romeo and Juliet, but there is the love that is so overpowering that it seems to transcend all bounds of convention and reason. This type of love, experienced by Romeo and Juliet, is the opposite of the restricted, courtly love that is prevalent in fourteenth century Verona. Courtly love was governed by the customs and traditions of the time. According to custom, the young man must ask the father for the hand of his daughter in marriage. There was no such thing as a "love" marriage because the marriages were arranged by the fathers. Girls were betrothed to whomever their fathers chose, usually in alliances for family betterment. Many times the girl was extremely young. Juliet was not quite fourteen, and her mother says that she herself married at that age. The arranged marriage was based on family status and kinship. By asking Lord Capulet for Juliet's hand in marriage, Paris abides by all the rules of etiquette and is in harmony with social expectations. On the other hand, Romeo will break all the conventional rules with his impulsiveness and his own values not subject to time or custom.

Study Questions

1. What is the setting for the play?

2. What scene of conflict opens the action of the play?

3. Which character tries to stop the fighting among the servants?

4. Which character is aggressive and eager to fight?

5. What warning does the Prince give to anyone who breaks the peace again?

6. Who has asked for Juliet's hand in marriage?

7. How old is Juliet?

8. In what state of mind is Romeo when we first see him in the play?

9. Explain how Romeo finds out about the Capulet ball.

10. How does Benvolio try to remedy Romeo's love sickness?

Answers

1. The setting is a street scene in Verona, Italy.

2. The play opens with a conflict between the Capulet and Montague servants. Eventually, even the townspeople become involved.

3. Benvolio tries to stop the fighting among the servants.

4. Tybalt is aggressive and eager to fight. He challenges Benvolio to draw his sword.

5. The Prince decrees that if anyone breaks the peace again, he shall pay with his life.

6. Paris has asked for Juliet's hand in marriage.

7. Juliet is thirteen years old.

8. As the play opens, Romeo's state of mind can best be described as love-sick, in love with love, moody, and melancholy.

9. Romeo finds out about the Capulet ball when an illiterate Capulet servant asks him to read the invitation list to him.

10. Benvolio tries to remedy Romeo's love-sickness by getting him to consent to go to the Capulet ball and examine other beauties.

Suggested Essay Topics

1. Explain the operation of fate and how it has worked in Scenes I and II of the play to help bring the two lovers together.

2. Explain the rules of marriage during the fourteenth century.

3. What major conflicts are established in the first scene?

4. Explain the purpose of the Prologue.

Act I, Scenes III–V (pages 12–22)

New Characters:

Nurse: *Juliet's nurse who has taken care of her since her infancy*

Susan: *the Nurse's daughter who was born on the same day as Juliet but died. She is not in the scene but is alluded to by the Nurse*

Mercutio: *a friend to Romeo who loves words*

Summary

In Scene III Lady Capulet informs Juliet that it is time for her to think of marriage. At first Lady Capulet sends the Nurse away, but then calls her back, remembering that she knows all their secrets anyway. The Nurse and Lady Capulet discuss Juliet's age; and the Nurse recalls exactly the hour of Juliet's birth because she was born on Lammas Eve, the same day as Susan, her daughter who died.

Lady Capulet asks Juliet if she is ready to marry. Juliet replies that she has not even thought of marriage. Lady Capulet tells her about Paris and compares him to a book that only needs a cover (a wife). Lady Capulet stresses his physical attractiveness and his wealth, which enforce the belief that love dwells in the eye rather than in the heart. Juliet, always obedient to her parents, agrees to look at him at the feast that night and to consider his suit.

Scene IV portrays Romeo and his friends on their way to the ball. The young men are carrying or wearing masks. Benvolio suggests that they enter quietly, dance, and then leave. Mercutio is a glib speaker and loves to hear himself talk. He is light-hearted and ridicules Romeo's love-sickness. He (Mercutio) delivers a speech about Queen Mab, the queen of fairyland, and what she is able to do to dreamers. Romeo has a premonition that something is about to happen that will shorten his life, but decides that he must go forward regardless.

The setting in Scene V is within the Capulet house. The servants are busy preparing for the ball. Lord Capulet, jolly and remembering his youth, welcomes everyone and intimidates the young women into dancing with him by saying that "Ladies that have their toes unplagued with corns will walk about (dance) with you." If any young lady refuses to dance with him, he swears to tell everyone that she has corns on her feet.

Romeo sees Juliet for the first time and falls instantly in love. His tortured love for Rosaline has been replaced with a blissful love for Juliet. He compares her beauty to the brightness of torches, a rich jewel in an Ethiop's ear, and a snowy dove. As he speaks of her beauty, Tybalt recognizes his voice and knows that he is a Montague. Tybalt sends for his sword only to be stopped by Lord Capulet, who warns him not to disrupt his ball with a fight. Lord Capulet allows Romeo to remain at the feast because he is behaving like a gentleman, Verona speaks well of him, and he does not want the joy of his ball disrupted. Tybalt is furious that Romeo is allowed to stay and storms out. Romeo and Juliet speak to one another using words such as "pilgrim," "saint," "palmers," "devotions," and "shrines"—all holy terms. Juliet is called away to her mother, and Romeo asks the Nurse who she is. He is told that she is a Capulet, and he realizes that his "life is my foe's debt." As Romeo and his friends leave the feast, Juliet asks the Nurse who he is. The Nurse tells her that "His name is Romeo, and a Montague, / The only son of your great enemy." It is this knowledge that makes Juliet say, "My only love sprung from my only hate! / Too early seen unknown, and known too late!"

Analysis

When Juliet's mother comes to discuss marriage with her and sends the Nurse away, the nurse feels disappointment and hurt. The Nurse has been more of a mother to Juliet than Lady Capulet. The Nurse and Lady Capulet are opposites in nature. The nurse exhibits complete ease with Juliet. She is earthy, a little bawdy, and very frank with her opinions, advice, and feelings. On the other hand, Lady Capulet is stiff and reserved with her daughter. Juliet responds to the Nurse with gaiety and fondness, while her relationship with her mother is reserved, respectful, and timid. Juliet is the child the Nurse took in when her own baby died; thus, a very close relationship has developed between the two. The ties between Juliet and the nurse go far beyond master and servant. Never discouraged by the Capulet family, the Nurse has taken on the role of companion, confidant, friend, mother, and co-conspirator.

It should be noted that Juliet is polite and obedient to her parents. Chastity, silence, and obedience were three virtues expected of both daughters and wives in the Elizabethan period. Juliet's defiance later in the play becomes a sign of the unconventionality of her love and its transforming powers. In Act I, Juliet respects the wishes of her parents and strives to please them, even if it means marrying someone they have chosen for her. When her mother discusses marriage with her, she is respectful, obedient, but indifferent. Her attitude will change as the play progresses and she becomes more of a woman.

Elizabethan spectators enjoyed humor, and Shakespeare does not disappoint them. Humor relieves tension built by intense moments in the script, and it also provides entertainment for the audience, especially the groundlings who might become restless if the action did not move rapidly. Shakespeare employs humor when old Lord Capulet, who is reliving his youth, threatens to tell everyone that any young lady who refuses to dance with him has corns on her feet. It is also used when Benvolio teases Romeo about his love-sickness. The Nurse's constant chatter when Lady Capulet tries to talk to Juliet about marriage, a serious subject, also provides additional humor in these scenes.

While humor and lightheartedness are important, images are equally important in building the total impression of the play, and these should be noted in the first act. As Lady Capulet appeals to Juliet to consider marriage to Paris, she uses the comparison of Paris to a fine book. Lady Capulet says, "Read o'er the volume of young Paris' face, and find delight writ there with beauty's pen.... And what obscur'd in this fair volume lies/ Find written in the margin of his eyes./ This precious book of love, this unbound lover,/ To beautify him only lacks a cover." The comparison is very formal and conventional.

The love that Romeo and Juliet share is sprinkled with religious imagery as well as light imagery. The words that Romeo and Juliet speak to one another upon first meeting are filled with religious meanings and undertones. The first 14 lines of their conversation is a sonnet consisting of references to worship. Juliet is the saint, and Romeo is the pilgrim. The imagery is illustrated with the following discussion between Romeo and Juliet. Romeo says, "If I profane with my unworthiest hand/ This holy shrine, the gentle fine is this:/My lips, two blushing pilgrims, ready stand/ To smooth that rough touch with a tender kiss." Juliet replies, "Good pilgrim, you do wrong your hand too much,/ Which mannerly devotion shows in this;/ For saints have hands that pilgrims' hands do touch,/ And palm to palm is holy palmers' kiss." The devotion that Romeo and Juliet show for one another is pure and holy, unlike the infatuation that he had felt so recently for Rosaline.

Throughout the play there is a contrast between light and dark images. Rosaline becomes associated with darkness and Juliet with lightness. The imagery of light is illustrated by such comparisons as Juliet's beauty to the brightness of torches, jewels, and a "snowy dove trooping with crows."

Mercutio is a key character in the play. He believes in taking action and in being realistic. He entertains his friends with his nimble wit and use of puns, figurative language, and word play. Mercutio's speech is both imaginative and filled with imagery as he describes the work of Queen Mab on sleeping people. He becomes carried away with his witty fantasy on dreams and has to be stopped by Romeo. Mercutio is used as a foil or contrast to Romeo. This contrast makes the particular qualities of each character stand out vividly. At this point in the play, Romeo is focused on his inner life and his emotions, while Mercutio is focused on entertaining others with his wit. Romeo is melancholy and fatalistic while Mercutio is cheerful and confident.

Through instances of chance, coincidence, circumstance, and change, the theme of fate in the lives of Romeo and Juliet is continued in Scenes III, IV, and V. Romeo was persuaded by Benvolio to attend the ball. He consents to go only to watch Rosaline, not knowing that he will meet his only true love—Juliet. Juliet, on the other hand, is present at the ball supposedly observing Paris, a prospective husband. Both Romeo and Juliet fall instantly in love with one another. It is also fate that Lord Capulet refuses to allow Tybalt to vent his anger against Romeo, and even allows Romeo to remain at the ball.

Foreshadowing anticipates what will come to pass, and thus reinforces the sense of fate at work in the play. There are three examples of foreshadowing in this act. The Prince's speech in Scene 1 warns that death will be the penalty if the city's peace is again disturbed by the feuding families. In Scene IV, Romeo has a premonition of something evil happening, "some consequence, yet hanging in the stars," but he feels that he can do nothing to prevent it from occurring. He believes that fate has complete control of his destiny and this premonition echoes the "star-crossed lovers" mentioned in the Prologue. The third example of foreshadowing is in Scene 5 when Tybalt delivers his warning as he leaves his uncle's feast. He states, "I will withdraw; but this intrusion shall,/ No seeming sweet, convert to bitt'rest gall." Tybalt vows to seek revenge upon Romeo for daring to attend the Capulet ball.

As a whole, Act I provides the reader with the introduction or exposition. It creates the tone of the play which allows the audience to know the dangers associated with a romance between a Capulet and a Montague. It presents the co-existing concepts of love and hate that are present not only within these two warring families, but in society at the time. Act I also defines the setting and introduces most of the characters.

Study Questions

1. Who is Susan?

2. When is Juliet's birthday?

3. Why does Lady Capulet visit with Juliet? What questions does she ask her?

4. How do the Nurse and Lady Capulet feel about Paris?

5. Which character loves to talk?

6. Who is Queen Mab?

7. What premonition does Romeo have?

8. How did Lord Capulet force the young ladies to dance with him?

9. Who recognizes Romeo's voice at the feast and becomes furious because he is allowed to stay?

10. Who first tells Romeo and Juliet who the other is?

Answers

1. Susan is the Nurse's daughter who was born on the same day as Juliet; however, she died.

2. Juliet's birthday is on Lammas Eve.

3. Lady Capulet visits with Juliet to ask her if she is ready for marriage. She asks Juliet to look at Paris at the feast that night.

4. The Nurse and Lady Capulet feel that Paris is a perfect match for Juliet and are in favor of the marriage.

5. Mercutio loves to talk and uses figurative language and many plays on words.

6. Queen Mab is the Queen of Fairies. She is responsible for what men dream.

7. Romeo has a premonition that something is about to happen that will shorten his life.

8. Lord Capulet threatens to tell everyone that any young lady who does not dance with him has corns on her feet.

9. Tybalt recognizes Romeo's voice and becomes furious when Lord Capulet allows him to remain at the ball.

10. The Nurse is the one who identifies each of the lovers.

Suggested Essay Topics

1. Compare the love that Romeo feels for Juliet to the love that he felt for Rosaline.

2. Explain the imagery of light and dark in Act I and how it is used as symbols for Rosaline and Juliet.

3. How does Shakespeare use humor in Act I?

4. Trace how fate has brought the two lovers together.

Act II

Act II, Scenes I and II (pages 23–30)

Summary

Act II begins with another Prologue in the form of a sonnet which provides the audience with a preview of what is to come. It states that the shallow love that Romeo had for Rosaline has been replaced with love for Juliet. "Alike bewitched by the charm of looks" expresses that both Romeo and Juliet are mutually attracted to one another. His feelings are returned and "passion lends them power."

Scene I takes place outside the walls of Lord Capulet's house. Romeo feels that he can not leave because his heart remains where Juliet lives, and he climbs over the wall into the orchard. Romeo's friends, who do not know of Romeo's new love, call for him and try to entreat him to come out of hiding by calling out Rosaline's name. Mercutio teases Romeo about Rosaline, not realizing that her name now means nothing to him. Romeo's friends give up looking for him and return to their homes.

Scene II takes place within the walls of Lord Capulet's orchard. Romeo watches as Juliet appears at her window and compares her to light, the East, the sun, and the stars in heaven. As she leans her cheek upon her hand, he wishes that he could be a glove on the hand that touches her cheek. He listens as she calls out his name, and he hears her proclaim that it is only his name that is her enemy. Romeo jumps from the bushes and declares that he will change his name if that is keeping her from loving him. Juliet is startled and surprised that he has heard her secret thoughts.

She asks how he was able to get over the high orchard walls and find her. To this, Romeo answers that love helped him accomplish both. Juliet is concerned that she has been too forward with him. She promises that she will be more true than any girl who acts shy and distant. Romeo tries to swear on the moon that he loves her; however, Juliet begs him not to swear on something that changes so frequently. The two lovers exchange vows of love, and Juliet asks if his intentions are honorable. If they are, when should she send someone to get the information concerning the time and place for their wedding. Romeo tells her to send someone at nine o'clock in the morning for the details. The Nurse calls to Juliet, interrupting their balcony love scene. As Romeo prepares to leave, Juliet says her famous lines, "Good night, good night! Parting is such sweet sorrow /That I shall say good night till it be morrow."

Analysis

These two scenes, which show that Benvolio and Mercutio believe Romeo is still playing a love game, and which isolate the lovers from family and friends, are probably the most well known scenes in the play. Some of the most poetic language is found here in the form of images, figures of speech, and the music of the lines.

Romeo's soliloquy, a dramatic monologue spoken aloud to reveal a the character's thoughts, is found in the first part of Scene II. The monologue conveys an idealized quality of their love and clearly describes his new feeling for Juliet in terms of brightness. He even states that the brightness of her eyes, if up in heaven, would light up the skies and make the birds think it was day. He again uses imagery of light and dark when he first sees Juliet on the balcony and states, "What light through yonder window breaks?/ It is the East, and Juliet is the sun!/Arise, fair sun, and kill the envious moon,/ Who is already sick and pale with grief." As Rosaline was compared to moon and night, Juliet is compared to sun, brightness, warmth, and light.

The famous lines, "O Romeo, Romeo! Wherefore art thou Romeo?" do not mean she is looking for him, but that she is asking why he is called Romeo and a Montague. She continues her speech declaring that if he cannot give up his name, she will give up her Capulet name. She then goes on to state that it is only his name that is her enemy, but not the person. She compares their love to lightning that ceases almost as soon as it is seen and to a bud that would bloom in time. This contrasting comparison illustrates the new meanings of love in each of their lives. Romeo is willing to face death in exchange for Juliet's love. The two lovers will repeatedly demonstrate that they prefer death to separation. Their entire relationship has been formed quickly. They have declared their love, exchanged vows, and plan to be married, all in a matter of hours. Possibly because both lovers realize the dangers of their love, they act quickly and impulsively.

Impulsive behavior is considered to be Romeo's tragic flaw (a weakness in a character that will cause his destruction). This flaw is first seen when Romeo quickly forgets Rosaline and turns his attentions to Juliet. He not only falls deeply in love with Juliet, but plans marriage, all within a matter of hours. While a certain amount of impetuosity is natural in the young, extremes can prove destructive for the characters.

Study Questions

1. Instead of returning home, where does Romeo go after the ball?

2. What is a soliloquy and how is it used in Scene II?

3. By whose name does Mercutio call for Romeo?

4. How does Romeo learn of Juliet's love for him?

5. What does Romeo say helped him climb over the high walls of the Capulet orchard and find Juliet's window?

6. What do Romeo and Juliet exchange?

7. What do Romeo and Juliet plan to do the next day?

8. To what does Romeo compare Juliet's beauty?

9. Who keeps interrupting the balcony scene?

10. Why does Juliet ask Romeo not to swear by the moon?

Answers

1. After the ball, Romeo goes over the wall and into the Capulet orchard.

2. A soliloquy is a dramatic monologue spoken aloud by a character to reveal his thoughts to the audience. Romeo uses a soliloquy to describe Juliet's beauty as she stands on her balcony.

3. Mercutio keeps calling for Romeo in Rosaline's name.

4. He overhears Juliet speaking of her love for him when she thinks she is alone.

5. Love, which gave him wings, helped him over the wall and made it possible for him to find her balcony.

6. Romeo and Juliet exchange vows of love.

7. Romeo and Juliet plan to be married the next day.

8. Romeo compares Juliet's beauty to brightness, warmth, and light.

9. The Nurse keeps interrupting the balcony scene.

10. Juliet asks Romeo not to swear his love on the moon because the moon appears to change in size as it orbits the earth, suggesting that it is fickle.

Suggested Essay Topics

1. Explain how imagery and figures of speech make Scene II one of the most beautiful scenes in the play. Describe the imagery and figures of speech and illustrate how they are used.

2. Explain the purpose of Scenes I and II.

3. Discuss Juliet's concerns in the balcony scene.

Act II, Scenes III and IV (pages 30–39)

New Characters:

Friar Laurence: *a Franciscan friar who is a priest and a specialist in herbs and medicines. He hopes that the marriage will end the feud between the two families.*

Peter: *the Nurse's servant*

Summary

As Scene III begins, the reader finds Friar Laurence carrying a wicker basket and selecting herbs, flowers, and plants to use in making medicine. It is daybreak on Monday, the second day in the lives of the lovers. Friar Laurence tells how plants contain both poisonous and healing powers. If a plant's use is abused, the result is harmful. "Virtue itself turns vice, being misapplied, / And vice sometime by action dignified." He applies this same lesson to man, who possesses both good and evil within him. If man allows the evil to become predominant in his life, it will destroy him.

Romeo approaches, and Friar Laurence asks if he is ill or if he has been up all night. Romeo answers that he has been up all night. To this, the Friar assumes that he has been with Rosaline and committed sin. Romeo assures him that this is not so and states that he has forgotten Rosaline. He reveals to the Friar that he has been with the daughter of Lord Capulet, and they have fallen in love and wish to be married today. The Friar scolds him for professing to love one woman one day and another on the next day. He states, "Young men's love then lies / Not truly in their hearts, but in their eyes." Romeo assures him that they both love one another. The Friar, hoping to end the feud by marrying the two lovers, agrees to marry them. As Romeo prepares to leave, the Friar worries about the haste of the marriage and says, "Wisely and slow. They stumble that run fast."

Scene 4 reveals Mercutio and Benvolio in the streets of Verona. They are discussing their love-sick friend who did not even go home last night after the ball. Benvolio says that Tybalt has sent a challenge to Romeo for a duel. Both friends wonder if Romeo will be able to handle a duel because he has been acting so strangely concerning Rosaline. His love-sickness has made him "already dead: stabbed with a white wench's black eye; run through the ear with a love song."

They are discussing Tybalt's expert fencing capabilities when Romeo appears. They tease Romeo about giving them the slip after the ball and about his love for Rosaline. As they banter words back and forth, the Nurse and her servant come on stage.

Mercutio makes fun of the Nurse with insulting words and she becomes angry. She asks for Romeo, and he identifies himself

to her. She says that Juliet has sent her for the marriage information. Romeo tells the Nurse that Juliet is to devise a reason to go to
chapel that evening, and Friar Laurence will marry them. Romeo
then tells her that his servant will give her a rope ladder to take back
with her. Romeo will use the ladder to climb into Juliet's window
later that night.

Analysis

Shakespeare's introduction of Friar Laurence gathering herbs
is especially important to the plot of the play. Elizabethans were
fascinated with potions and poisons, and the Friar's philosophical
discourse on the power of medicinal plants and the similarities
between plants and men enthralled them. The speech at the beginning of Scene 3 is a soliloquy stressing the dichotomy of nature
and man and could be viewed as foreshadowing. Man, like many
plants, does possess the capability of evil as well as good. Even
the goodness in Romeo cannot overshadow his feelings of revenge
later in the play. The Friar himself attempts to accomplish good by
agreeing to unite the lovers in marriage, hoping that the alliance
will end the feud between the families. Yet, the Friar acts rashly or
impulsively when he agrees to the marriage. His intentions are good
and honorable; however, he acts without considering the possible
consequences of a secret marriage between members of feuding
families. He cautions Romeo by saying that "Wisely and slow; they
stumble that run fast." Then, he violates his own admonition by
hastily agreeing to the marriage. Friar Laurence's hastiness is also
a flaw within him that will aid in the destruction of the lovers.

Romeo's tragic flaw, impulsiveness, is recognized by the Friar
who cautions him about acting too hastily. He reminds Romeo of
his infatuation with Rosaline, which is so quickly forgotten. The
Friar is an understanding and broadminded man who only tries
to help by agreeing to the marriage.

Mercutio is again illustrated as a man of many words as he
teases Romeo about Rosaline and love. As Mercutio and Benvolio discuss Romeo and the challenge sent by Tybalt, Mercutio is
concerned about Romeo's ability to fight. "Alas, poor Romeo, he is
already dead! / Stabb'd with a white wench's black eye; shot through
/ The ear with a love song; the very pin of his heart / Cleft with the

blind bow-boy's butt-shaft; and is he / A man to encounter Tybalt?" Mercutio has no idea that Romeo is no longer bothered with his former infatuation with Rosaline or that he has moved on to a new and deeper relationship with Juliet.

When the Nurse and Peter arrive upon the streets of Verona, Mercutio enjoys ridiculing her as well. She, in turn, reveals coarseness or vulgarity by saying, "I'll take him down,/ And 'a were lustier than he is, and twenty / Such Jacks; and if I cannot, I'll find those that shall./ Scurvy knave!" When she talks to Romeo, she tries to appear more ladylike by saying "I desire some confidence with you." She should have said, "conference." The use of a word that sounds like the one intended but is ridiculously wrong is called a malapropism and is used by Shakespeare in many of the Nurse's speeches.

The Nurse's love for Juliet prompts her to warn Romeo against hurting her. The Nurse plays an important part in advancing the plot of the play. She is closest to Juliet and enjoys being a part of the romantic plans of marriage. She is the important messenger of the details of the union, of when and where it will take place.

By the second day, the lovers have met, fallen in love, and plan to marry. The lovers are able to accomplish this with the help of the Nurse and the Friar, who have become accomplices.

Study Questions

1. What is Friar Laurence's special skill or area of knowledge?

2. With what does Friar Laurence compare the beneficial and poisonous parts of the plant?

3. About what does the Friar caution Romeo?

4. Why does the Friar agree to marry Romeo and Juliet?

5. Who has sent Romeo a challenge for a duel?

6. What excuse is Juliet to give for going to Friar Laurence's cell?

7. Where are Romeo and Juliet to be married?

8. Who teases Romeo about Rosaline and his love-sickness?

9. Who teases the Nurse and causes her to become crass?

10. How does Romeo plan to get into Juliet's window?

Answers

1. Friar Laurence's special skill is in making medicines and potions from herbs.

2. Friar Laurence compares the beneficial and poisonous parts of a plant to the good and evil within a man.

3. Friar Laurence cautions Romeo about being too hasty.

4. The Friar believes that by marrying the two lovers, he will end the feud between the Capulets and the Montagues.

5. Tybalt has sent Romeo a challenge for a duel. He is angry that Romeo came to the ball uninvited and was allowed to remain.

6. Juliet is going to get permission to go to Friar Laurence's cell by saying that she needs to go to shrift, or confession.

7. Romeo and Juliet are to be married in Friar Laurence's cell.

8. Mercutio, Romeo's friend, teases him about Rosaline and his love-sickness.

9. Mercutio teases the Nurse and causes her to become angry.

10. Romeo has given the Nurse a rope ladder in order that he might climb into Juliet's window later that night.

Suggested Essay Topics

1. Name the two other people in the play who know about the love between Romeo and Juliet and explain how they help the lovers achieve their goals.

2. Explain Friar Laurence's philosophy concerning the parts of a plant as compared to the potential actions of man.

3. Describe Mercutio and his role in the play.

Act II, Scenes V and VI (pages 39–42)

Summary

Scene V takes place within the Capulet orchard where Juliet is anxiously waiting for the Nurse to return with news from Romeo. The Nurse left at nine o'clock and it is now twelve. Juliet wishes that the Nurse were as in love as she is so that she would be faster in her return, for the waiting is torture for Juliet. The Nurse finally arrives, and Juliet says, "O Lord, why lookest thou sad? / Though news be sad, yet tell them merrily; / If good, thou shamest the music of sweet news / By playing it to me with so sour a face." The Nurse replies that her bones ache and asks that Juliet leave her alone for awhile. Juliet says, "I would thou hadst my bones, and I thy news." The Nurse banters with Juliet, claiming to be hot and too tired to talk. Then she tells Juliet that she has made a good choice. The Nurse finally asks Juliet if she is able to go to shrift today. If so, Romeo is waiting there to make her his wife.

Scene VI takes place in Friar Laurence's cell where both he and Romeo are waiting for the arrival of Juliet. The Friar hopes that the future will not punish them with sorrow, and Romeo replies that sorrow cannot equal the joy that one minute in the sight of Juliet gives him. The Friar again cautions Romeo with the words, "Love moderately; long love doth so; Too swift arrives as tardy as too slow."

Juliet arrives and they both proclaim their immense love for one another. Juliet says, "But my true love is grown to such excess / I cannot sum up sum of half my wealth." At this point, the Friar performs the wedding ceremony.

Analysis

The love scenes are brought to a resolution as the friar marries the two lovers at the end of Scene VI. The relationship is further strengthened between Juliet and the Nurse as the nurse teases her about the wedding plans sent by Romeo. The Nurse is more the mother than Juliet's real mother—Lady Capulet. The nurse is immersed in Juliet's affairs and strives to help her with her plans. She approves of Romeo—his good looks and his polite mannerisms.

It is almost humorous the way Shakespeare allows the Nurse to torment Juliet with her important news. "Now, good sweet nurse—O Lord, why look'st thou sad?/ Though news be sad, yet tell them merrily;/ If good, thou shamest the music of sweet news/ By playing it to me with so sour a face." The nurse replies, "I am aweary, give me leave awhile./ Fie, how my bones ache! What a jounce have I had!" Juliet says, " I would thou hadst my bones, and I thy news." As she complains about her weary bones, her tiredness, and her headache, Juliet is impatient to learn if and when she will be a bride.

The actual marriage ceremony is not included in the text. The beauty of the moment is presented as Romeo and Juliet exchange their love for one another, and the Friar states, "You shall not stay alone/ Till Holy Church incorporate two in one."

There was no such thing as a "love" marriage in the Elizabethan social culture. The marriages were arranged by the father, and the daughter was expected to be obedient to her parents in their requests. It should be noted that Paris was courting by the accepted rules of the day. He talked with the father first and asked for Juliet's hand in marriage. Paris is patient and waits for an answer from Lord Capulet. Romeo, on the other hand, does not court by the accepted rules. He has gone behind the father's back, talked directly with the daughter, and asks her to marry him. Not only has he not courted by the rules, the lovers are married secretly without the knowledge or consent of the parents.

It should also be noted that Juliet, like Romeo, is impatient and hasty in her decisions. She has abandoned all sense of reason and propriety and is ruled entirely by her impulses. She has fallen in love within the space of only a few hours and plans to marry within one day of meeting Romeo. Her impatience is also shown as she waits for the Nurse to return from seeing Romeo and again as she inquires about the meeting between the two.

Time, newly calculated or experienced in love's world is referred to in Juliet's soliloquy as she waits for the Nurse to return with the wedding news. Love has made time of great importance. Juliet's impatience and hastiness is illustrated as she waits for the Nurse to return from meeting with Romeo. She states, "Therefore do nimble-pinio'd doves draw Love,/ And therefore hath the wind-swift Cupid wings./ Now is the sun upon the highmost hill/ Of this day's journey, and from nine till twelve/ Is three long hours; yet she is not come." Time has new meaning for Juliet. The love that she feels is unconventional and not a part of the regimented society of Verona.

Romeo has plunged into his new love impulsively. His passions completely absorb him and he has no thoughts of the consequences of his love for Juliet. His actions are not guided by reason, but by feelings alone. His willingness to face death is again acknowledged when Romeo states, "Then love-devouring death do what he dare—/ It is enough I may but call her mine." He does not realize that his lines touch upon the theme of love co-existing with death, or that they foreshadow the future for him and his new love.

Act II is where the complication or rising action takes place. Tension is created because of the conflict created when the children of two opposing families meet and fall in love. Additional conflicts are presented in the form of Tybalt challenging Romeo to a duel, and the actual marriage of Romeo and Juliet performed by Friar Laurence. This marriage intensifies the conflict, which in turn adds to the complication of Act II.

Study Questions

1. At what time did Juliet send the Nurse to see Romeo and find out the wedding plans?

2. How long has Juliet been waiting for the Nurse to return with the news from Romeo?

3. How does the Nurse react when she finally returns?

4. How does the Nurse feel about the marriage?

5. What is the Friar afraid of?

6. The friar warns Romeo again about something. What is it?

7. How much do the lovers say their love has grown?

8. How many people know of the marriage?

9. Where does the marriage take place?

10. What is another name for the Friar?

Answers

1. Juliet sent the Nurse at nine o'clock in the morning to find out the wedding news from Romeo.

2. Juliet has been waiting three hours for the Nurse to return with the news.

3. The Nurse teases Juliet by claiming to be tired from her journey and prolongs telling her the news.

4. The Nurse is in favor of the marriage and feels that Romeo is handsome as well as polite.

5. The Friar is afraid that both lovers are acting too hastily.

6. The Friar warns Romeo again about acting too hastily.

7. The lovers say that their love has grown to such an extent that it cannot be counted.

8. Four main characters know of the marriage. Romeo and Juliet, of course, are aware; but also the Nurse and Friar Laurence have become accomplices in the affair.

9. The marriage takes place in Friar Laurence's cell or chapel.

10. Friar Laurence is also referred to as the ghostly confessor.

Suggested Essay Topics

1. Explain the relationship between the Nurse and Juliet.

2. Explain the rules of courtship during this time period. Compare and contrast the actions of Paris and of Romeo in regard to courting and marriage.

3. Friar Laurence plays an important role in the lives of Romeo and Juliet. Explain his role in their lives—his concerns and his hopes.

SECTION FOUR

Act III

Act III, Scenes I and II (pages 43–52)

Summary

Scene I takes place on the streets of Verona. It is Monday afternoon on day two, about an hour after the wedding between Romeo and Juliet. Benvolio and Mercutio are walking down one of the streets when Benvolio suggests that they retire. The day is extremely hot, and if they meet with the Capulets, tempers will flare and there is bound to be a fight. Mercutio is ready for a fight and hopes to have one. The Capulets enter led by Tybalt, who inquires about Romeo. Tybalt had challenged Romeo to a duel to get revenge for his uninvited appearance at the Capulet ball. At this time, Romeo, who is returning from Friar Laurence's chapel, approaches the group of men.

Tybalt insults Romeo by calling him a villain, but Romeo responds by saying that Tybalt does not know him. To this, Tybalt challenges him to draw his sword, but Romeo replies, "I do protest I never injured thee, But love thee better than thou canst devise." Mercutio steps in to defend Romeo's honor and returns Tybalt's insult by calling him "Good King of Cats." Mercutio draws and he and Tybalt begin to fight. Romeo calls for Benvolio to help him stop the fight. Romeo reaches to push Mercutio away, thereby blocking Mercutio's view. Tybalt takes the opportunity to reach under Romeo's arm and fatally stabs Mercutio. When Romeo is told that Mercutio is dead, he realizes that his love for Juliet has made him act "effeminately." When Mercutio is killed, Romeo's sense of honor and loyalty leave him no choice but to avenge his friend's death. He calls to Tybalt who returns and they fight. Romeo kills Tybalt and immediately realizes that he has murdered his new bride's cousin. Benvolio pleads with him to run and hide before he is found. The Prince comes to the public square and asks Benvolio the cause of the deaths. Benvolio relates the story, and the Prince exiles Romeo under penalty of death.

Scene II takes place late Monday afternoon. Juliet is anxiously waiting for night to come and with it, Romeo. The Nurse enters carrying the rope ladder and crying, "He's dead, he's dead, he's dead...O Romeo, Romeo! / Who ever would have thought it? Romeo!" Juliet mistakenly thinks that Romeo is dead. Then the Nurse begins calling out Tybalt's name and Juliet believes that both Romeo and Tybalt are dead. The Nurse finally tells her that Romeo killed Tybalt and has been banished by the Prince. Juliet, at first, feels betrayed by Romeo. Then her love for Romeo takes away the blame she felt against him. Juliet tells the Nurse that she will be weeping long after others have stopped weeping for Tybalt. She orders the Nurse to take a ring to Romeo as a token and to bid him come to her that night for a last farewell.

Analysis

Act I of the play is considered the introduction with Act II being the complication or rising action. Act III of the play is the climax or turning point. The turning point of a play takes place when something happens that turns the action of the play either toward a happy ending or toward a tragic ending. Romeo's killing of Tybalt is the turning point. Because of this act, Romeo will be banished, and there is no chance that he and Juliet will be able to reveal their marriage to their feuding parents. After the murders take place, the fate of the lovers is really out of their hands. Circumstances just carry the lovers into destruction and hopelessness.

Many of the characters have unknowingly aided in the rapidly approaching destruction of the lovers. Friar Laurence has contributed by hastily consenting to marry them without thinking about the consequences. The Nurse, through love for Juliet and her enjoyment of the "love game," has also contributed to the tragedy. Tybalt, because of his temper and unwillingness to have Romeo remain at the Capulet ball, issued a challenge, which led to the inevitability of a duel. Even Romeo's preoccupation with Juliet and his love contribute to reaching the climax of the play. These characters are all involved in the downfall of the lovers. However, none of them do so diliberately. Their basic character traits cause them to act and react in the manner that they do. While fate still has some role in these events, it is important to acknowledge that action proceeds inevitably from the nature of the characters and the conditions surrounding them.

Shakespeare has created three distinct personalities in the characters of Tybalt, Benvolio, and Mercutio. All the young men involved in the quarrel have contrasting temperaments. Tybalt is arrogant, proud, bad-tempered, and is called "Good King of Cats." Benvolio, on the other hand, is reasonable, offers good will to all, and is peace loving. It is interesting to note that he is the one who always tries to make peace, break up fights, and console his friends. It is Benvolio who relates to Lord Montague the details of the initial fight in the beginning of the play, and it is Benvolio who is asked by the Prince to relate the details of this deadly fight in Act III, Scene 1. Mercutio is portrayed as clever; smart; and a lover of words, puns, and figures of speech. He is able to joke even about death. When Mercutio is asked about his wound, he replies with a pun, a humorous use of a word to suggest two or more meanings, by stating, "No, 'tis not so deep as a well, nor so wide / as a church door; but 'tis enough, 'twill serve. Ask / for me tomorrow, and you shall find me a grave man." He is, in fact, so witty that no one takes him seriously when he is no longer joking.

Fate or chance again comes into play when the Prince gives Romeo his sentence. The law of Verona declares that if someone sheds blood, then his blood must be shed also. Because Tybalt killed Mercutio, he himself must be killed, and Romeo accomplished just that. However, Romeo has then shed blood. The Prince could have Romeo put to death, but he only banishes him.

The Nurse, in Scene II, again misleads Juliet by not immediately telling her the news of Tybalt and Romeo. She weeps and cries out names and keeps Juliet guessing what has actually happened. The Nurse does not intentionally attempt to keep the news from Juliet, but she is overcome with grief. Her nature prevents her from telling Juliet the news in a calm and straightforward manner. When

Juliet first hears that Romeo is responsible for Tybalt's death, she feels deceived by his love. She answers the Nurse using oxymorons, "O serpent heart, hid with a flow'ring face!/ Did ever dragon keep so fair a cave?/ Beautiful tyrant! fiend angelical!/ Dove-feather'd raven! wolvish-ravening lamb!/ Despised substance of divinest show!/ Just opposite to what thou justly seem'st—/ A damned saint, an honourable villain!"

Juliet has divided emotions between her cousin and her husband, but when the nurse wishes grief, woes, and sorrows upon Romeo, Juliet rallies to Romeo's defense with the words, "Blister'd be thy tongue/ For such a wish! He was not born to shame. / Upon his brow shame is asham'd to sit;/ For 'tis a throne where honour may be crown'd/ Sole monarch of the universal earth." Juliet immediately realizes that her allegiance is with her husband. Even though she feels betrayed by him, she loves him deeply. Her love for him transcends even the grief of her cousin's death.

There is an ironic juxtaposition of love and death in these scenes. The values of love are represented by their marriage. This new love has caused Romeo to behave differently in the face of Tybalt's challenge and insults. And, set against this emotional love and well-being is the atmosphere of hate and revenge. After the death of Mercutio, Romeo realizes that his love has replaced his masculine characteristics. This leaves him feeling that he betrayed Mercutio by allowing him to fight what should have been his own fight. He states, "O sweet Juliet,/ Thy beauty hath made me effeminate/ And in my temper soft'ned valour's steel!" After the death of his friend, Romeo replaces his effeminate values of love with the masculine values of honor and revenge.

Shakespeare uses a number of allusions in this play, many of which are found in Scene II as Juliet waits for Romeo to come to her by night. Allusion is a reference to something in another work of literature, mythology, or history, and it is illustrated in the references to Phoebus Apollo, the Greek and Roman god of light.

Many examples of the theme of light and dark recur in these scenes. As Juliet is anxiously waiting for Romeo to come to her in scene 2, she gives a poetic praise of night when she states, "Come, night; come, Romeo; come, thou day in night;/ For thou wilt lie upon the wings of night/ Whiter than new snow upon a raven's back./ Come, gentle night; come, loving, black-brow'd night;/ Give me my Romeo; and, when he shall die,/ Take him and cut him out in little stars,/ And he will make the face of heaven so fine/ That all the world will be in love with night/ And pay no worship to the garish sun." The romantic night will give her her love who is illustrated as the brightness in the realm of blackness. Along with the images of dark and light is the reference to love and death co-existing side by side. Even in death, Juliet knows that he will continue to light the heavens in the form of stars.

Study Questions

1. Who begs Mercutio to leave the streets of Verona because the Capulets might also be out on this extremely hot day?

2. Who comes to the public square looking for a fight with Romeo?

3. What does Mercutio call Tybalt?

4. How does Tybalt insult Romeo and try to get him to fight him?

5. Why won't Romeo fight Tybalt?

6. Why does Mercutio fight Tybalt?

7. How is Mercutio killed?

8. Why does Romeo kill Tybalt?

9. Who tells the Prince about the murders?

10. What is Romeo's punishment?

Answers

1. Benvolio tries to get Mercutio to leave the streets of Verona because he is trying to prevent another fight.

2. Tybalt comes to the public square hoping to incite a fight with Romeo.

3. Mercutio calls Tybalt "Good King of Cats."

4. Tybalt insults Romeo by calling him a villain, hoping that this will cause him to fight.

5. Romeo will not fight Tybalt because now they are related by marriage. Tybalt is Juliet's cousin.

6. Mercutio fights Tybalt because he is angry that Tybalt is insulting Romeo, his friend.

7. Mercutio is killed when Romeo comes between them and blocks his view of Tybalt. Tybalt reaches under Romeo's arm and stabs Mercutio.

8. Romeo kills Tybalt because he feels that he must revenge his friend's death. After all, it was Romeo's fight and not Mercutio's.

9. Benvolio is the one who tells the Prince about the murders and relates exactly what happened.

10. Romeo's punishment is to be banished from Verona. If he is caught in the city of Verona, he will be put to death.

Suggested Essay Topics

1. Describe the events that foreshadow the death of Tybalt.

2. Define pun and explain how it is used in this act.

3. Act III is considered the climax of the plot. Explain why this is so.

4. Describe the character of Mercutio and the part he plays in the life of Romeo.

Act III, Scenes III and IV (pages 53–59)

Summary

Scene III takes place on Monday night inside Friar Laurence's cell. When Romeo fled the streets of Verona after the killings, he went there to hide. As the Friar approaches, the distraught Romeo asks what the Prince has decreed as his punishment.

The Friar says, "Not body's death, but body's banishment." To this, Romeo cries that banishment is worse than death because "There is no world without Verona walls." Friar Laurence attempts to make Romeo realize that he could have been sentenced to death, that the decree of banishment means that at least he will live. Romeo claims that not being able to see and touch Juliet is the same punishment as death. Romeo will not be consoled and throws himself on the floor in an extravagant display of grief.

The Nurse enters and is stern with Romeo. She says, "Stand up, stand up! Stand, and you be a man. / For Juliet's sake, for her sake, rise and stand! / Why should you fall into so deep an O?" At the sound of Juliet's name, Romeo inquires about her and asks if she hates him for killing her cousin. The nurse says that she is weeping and calling out both their names. Romeo grabs a knife, asks where in his anatomy does the name Montague lodge, and attempts to kill himself by cutting out that part.

The Nurse takes the dagger from Romeo, and the Friar accuses him of being womanish. The Friar gives Romeo three reasons why he should be glad that he is alive. One, Juliet is alive. Two, Tybalt could have killed him instead of the other way around. He should be happy that he (Romeo) is alive. Three, the Prince exiled Romeo instead of ordering his death. Friar Laurence then suggests a plan. Romeo is to visit Juliet that night as planned earlier. Then, he is to leave the city before daylight and travel to Mantua where he will stay until it is safe to return to Verona. The Friar will attempt to reconcile the feuding families, reveal the secret marriage, and obtain the Prince's pardon for Romeo which will allow him to return to Verona. The Nurse and Romeo are pleased with the plan. She gives Romeo Juliet's ring. The Friar warns Romeo once again that he must be out of the city before the break of day. Friar Laurence will keep in touch with Romeo through his servant and let him know how things are progressing in Verona.

Scene IV takes place within the Capulet house where the reader finds Paris evidently asking for an answer to his suit of marriage to Juliet. Lord and Lady Capulet are present, and it is very late on Monday night. Lord Capulet tells Paris that under the circumstances of the day (the recent killings) they have not had the opportunity to discuss marriage with Juliet. Lord Capulet, thinking that Juliet will be obedient in his wishes, decides to go ahead and tell Paris that he will give his consent for them to marry on Thursday of that week. Lord Capulet asks Lady Capulet to tell Juliet the good news before she retires for bed.

Analysis

Both Romeo and Juliet view his banishment as the worse kind of punishment. When Friar Laurence tells him the Prince's decree, Romeo states, "There is no world without Verona walls,/ But purgatory, torture, hell itself./ Hence-banished is banish'd from the world,/ And world's exile is death: then banished,/ Is death misterm'd; calling death banishment." Romeo realizes that his name has caused most of the complications in his life. Had his name not been Montague, he and Juliet could possibly have married with the blessings of both sets of parents. His anguish over killing Juliet's cousin causes him to become irrational. He draws his sword and states, "In what vile part of this anatomy/ Doth my name lodge? tell me that I may sack / The hateful mansion."

The Friar keeps Romeo from killing himself, but Romeo's attempted suicide is another example of his impulsiveness. He is very emotional and very rash in everything he does. His love with Juliet has been intense and fast and now appears to be destroyed. The love that he and Juliet share seems to be all consuming for both of them. It is not a courtly love and is not even considered a part of this world. Their love is so overwhelming that neither can imagine existing without the other. Death becomes the solution if they cannot be together.

The Nurse and Friar Laurence accept the news of death and banishment differently. True to her character, the Nurse is incoherent as she relates the news of Tybalt to Juliet; however, the Friar remains calm and philosophical concerning Romeo. These two characters begin to take on an even greater role in the lives of the lovers as they attempt to help and comfort them. It is the Friar who comes up with a plan to reunite the lovers for one last time. Friar Laurence only wants to help the lovers and ultimately end the feuding between the families. The Friar also realizes that he plays an important part in the consequences of the hastily arranged marriage performed by him. He must feel responsible for what has ultimately happened. His chances of reuniting the warring families looks rather bleak at this time.

The plot becomes intricate and complicated when Lord Capulet agrees to the marriage suit of Paris. He tells Paris, "I will make a desperate tender/ Of my child's love; I think she will be ruled/ In all respects by me; nay, more, I doubt it not." This announcement is not only significant for plot, but is an expression of patriarchal values, which are set against the freedom of love. Just as Romeo becomes a victim of societal values based on revenge and honor, so Juliet must submit to patriarchal authority in which women are always in subjection to their husbands or fathers. He has no idea that Juliet is already married, but assumes that she will be obedient to him and his requests. The customs of the day required her complete obedience. By arranging the marriage for Thursday, he unknowingly will force Juliet into more hasty actions. The plans of her father add new complications to Juliet's already troubled life.

Dramatic irony occurs when the audience knows that Juliet and Romeo are already married, and the characters on stage have no idea. Even as Lord Capulet gives his consent to Paris, they do not know that Romeo is with Juliet in her chamber.

Study Questions

1. What day is it in Scene III?

2. Where did Romeo run to hide after the murder of Tybalt?

3. How does he react to the news that he is banished from Verona?

4. Who tells him that the Prince has banished him?

5. What upsets Romeo the most about being banished?

6. The Friar gives three reasons that Romeo should be happy. What were they?

7. What does the Nurse give to Romeo?

8. Where is Romeo to go before daybreak?

9. On what day does Lord Capulet plan for Juliet to be married to Paris?

10. Who is to tell Juliet the "good news" concerning her future marriage to Paris?

Answers

1. It is very late on Monday night in Scene 3.

2. After the murders, Romeo ran to hide in Friar Laurence's cell.

3. Romeo would rather die than be banished from Verona.

4. The Friar tells him the news that he will not be killed but only banished.

5. The thought of not seeing or touching Juliet ever again bothers Romeo the most.

6. The Friar gives Romeo three reasons for being happy: Juliet is alive; he is alive, and he is only banished not killed.

7. The Nurse gives Juliet's ring to Romeo.

8. Romeo must leave Juliet's bed chamber before daybreak and go to Mantua.

9. Lord Capulet has arranged for Juliet to marry Paris on Thursday.

10. Lady Capulet is to tell Juliet the "good news" before she retires to bed.

Suggested Essay Topics

1. Discuss Friar Laurence's plan to reunite Romeo and Juliet.

2. The nurse and Friar Laurence react differently to the situations presented in these scenes. Compare and contrast these reactions.

3. What events take place that complicate Juliet's life?

Act III, Scene V (pages 59–66)

Summary

    Scene V takes place very early Tuesday morning on day three. Romeo and Juliet have been together for the night and are discussing whether they hear the nightingale or the lark. The nightingale sings at night, and the lark sings in early morning. The child in Juliet insists that it is the nightingale, while Romeo insists that it is the lark, and he must hurry from the city. Juliet persuades him that it is the nightingale, and Romeo decides that he will stay longer, risking capture and even death. At this point, the more mature and fearful Juliet says that it is indeed the lark, and he must flee. They bid farewell, and Juliet has a vision that the next time that they see one another, he will be dead in a tomb.

Romeo leaves and Lady Capulet enters. Juliet is surprised by her mother's early visit and allows her mother to believe that her red eyes and wan appearance are the result of her weeping for Tybalt. Lady Capulet tells Juliet that she is going to send someone to Mantua to give Romeo poison. Then she tells her that she has good news for her. Her father has agreed to have her marry County Paris at Saint Peter's Church next Thursday.

Juliet says, "He shall not make me there a joyful bride!" Lord Capulet enters and notices the tears and asks if Lady Capulet has given her the news. Lady Capulet assures him that she told Juliet the news, and she (Juliet) wants nothing to do with Paris or the marriage.

Lord Capulet threatens Juliet and tells her that she will marry him or she can beg on the streets for all he cares, but she will inherit nothing from him. Juliet begs him for a delay, but he is angry and strong willed with her. He tells her that she will be at the church on Thursday even if he has to drag her there on a hurdle.

Juliet turns to her mother for help, and Lady Capulet says, "Do as thou wilt, for I have done with thee." When Lord and Lady Capulet leave, she turns to the nurse for help. The advice of the Nurse is to forget Romeo because he is banished. She recommends that Juliet marry Paris, who is "a lovely gentleman." To this advice, Juliet tells the Nurse that she is going to Friar Laurence's cell to make confession and be forgiven for her sins. Juliet is really going to seek his advice. If the Friar can not help her out of this situation, she has the power to kill herself rather than marry Paris.

Analysis

Within a matter of two days, Juliet has grown from an obedient child into a willful young woman. As morning comes after their wedding night together Juliet at first refuses to believe that it is the lark singing, because she cannot bear to have Romeo leave her. Knowing that the lark sings at daybreak, and the nightingale sings at night, she wants to forestall daybreak when she knows that Romeo must leave. When Romeo says, "Let me be taken, let me be put to death," she becomes practical and aware of the danger. She then considers his safety before her desires and knows that it is time for him to leave. As Romeo leaves and she is looking down at him in the dawn of light, she says, "O God, I have an ill-divining soul!/ Methinks I see thee, now thou art below,/ As one dead in the bottom of a tomb;/ Either my eyesight fails, or thou look'st pale." Her premonition is a foreshadowing of the events to come.

The discussion between Lord and Lady Capulet and Juliet is extremely revealing. It allows the reader to see the coldness that exists between Juliet and her mother. There seems to be no closeness whatsoever. When Lady Capulet tells Juliet's father that she wants nothing to do with the marriage to Paris, Lord Capulet becomes angry. Juliet's mother tells him that "I would the fool were married to her grave!" Little did she know that she was foreshadowing the future for her daughter. Juliet pleads with her mother to help her delay the marriage, and her mother turns from her. Juliet attempts to persuade Lord Capulet to delay the marriage which causes him to become almost violent with her. He says, "Hang thee, young baggage! Disobedient wretch! / I tell thee what—get thee to church a Thursday / Or never after look me in the face. / Speak not, reply not, do not answer me! / My fingers itch." He goes on to rant and rave that she can beg, starve or die in the streets because he wants nothing to do with her if she does not consent to the marriage to Paris. He uses such insulting names as "greensickness," "carrion," "baggage," and "tallow-face" to describe his daughter. These are hardly words of endearment coming from her father. He cannot comprehend her disobeying him and is outraged at her sudden defiance.

Juliet delivers a brief soliloquy at the end of Act III as she expresses anger with the Nurse and announces that she will go consult with the Friar. Up until this point, the Nurse has been Juliet's confidant, counselor, and conspirator in her plans; however, her advice to marry Paris and forget Romeo has caused Juliet to seek help from someone else. By advising Juliet to forget Romeo and marry Paris, the Nurse totally loses Juliet's confidence. Juliet will no longer confide in the Nurse or trust her. She has also enabled Juliet to become more independent and self-reliant.

By the end of Act III, both Romeo and Juliet have changed a great deal. Both lovers realize that the love that they have for one another is beyond this world of customs and parental involvement. Their love goes even beyond death, and they never waver in their fidelity. Rashness is still considered Romeo's tragic flaw. It is not his desire for revenge but the rashness of the revenge that was his undoing. Juliet's changes are demonstrated in her new determination and strength of character as she goes alone to Friar Laurence to seek advice.

Study Questions

1. On what day does Scene V take place?

2. What is significant about the lark and the nightingale?

3. What vision does Juliet have as Romeo is leaving?

4. Who comes to visit with Juliet early that morning?

5. What news does Lady Capulet give to Juliet?

6. What is Juliet's reaction to the news that Lady Capulet gives her?

7. Who does Juliet turn to for help when her parents leave?

8. What advice does the Nurse give Juliet?

9. Why does Juliet tell the Nurse that she is going to see Friar Laurence?

10. If the Friar cannot furnish a solution for Juliet, what does she have the power to do?

Answers

1. Scene V takes place on day three, a Tuesday morning.

2. The lovers are trying to determine the time of night or early morning. Romeo must be out of the city before daylight. The nightingale sings at night, while the lark sings in the early part of the morning.

3. Juliet has a vision that she sees Romeo as one dead in the bottom of a tomb.

4. Juliet's mother, Lady Capulet, comes to visit with her early that morning.

5. Lady Capulet brings Juliet the news that her father has consented for her to marry Paris on Thursday.

6. Juliet is upset and willfully says that she will not marry Paris. This is the first time she has been disobedient to her parents.

7. After her parents leave, Juliet turns to the Nurse for a solution to her dilemma.

8. The Nurse advises Juliet to forget Romeo, since he is banished, and marry Paris.

9. Juliet tells the Nurse that she is going to see Friar Laurence to confess her sins and get forgiveness. She is really going there to seek the Friar's help.

10. If Friar Laurence cannot help her, she has the power to commit suicide rather than marry Paris.

Suggested Essay Topics

1. Explain the relationship between Juliet and her parents. How has it changed from the beginning of the play?

2. Explain how Juliet has changed from the beginning of Act I up until Act III. Give examples of her behavior then and now.

3. Describe the role of the Nurse in Juliet's life. How does this role change in Act III?

4. What event forms the climax or turning point of the play, and what complications does this event create for Romeo and Juliet?

Act IV

Act IV, Scenes I–III (pages 67–73)

Summary

As Scene I opens, Paris is found at Friar Laurence's cell consulting with him about his wedding plans. The friar, who knows why this marriage can never take place, says that it is rushing to have the marriage on Thursday. Paris tells Friar Laurence that they have decided to go ahead and marry because Juliet has been weeping uncontrollably, and her father is worried about her. Lord Capulet, not knowing that she weeps for Romeo, believes that the marriage will help her get over Tybalt's death more quickly. Juliet arrives and Paris greets her as his wife. She responds coolly but cordially. After Paris tells her that he will come for her early Thursday morning, he departs. Juliet entreats the Friar to "come weep with me—past hope, past care, past help!"

The Friar tells her that he already knows the circumstances. Juliet explains that she would do anything to get out of the marriage to Paris and pleads for the friar to help her. She also tells him that if he cannot help, she will kill herself rather than marry Paris.

The Friar, realizing that she is serious about her feelings, tells her that he has a plan. She must go home, consent to marry Paris, and then she is to sleep alone on that Wednesday night before the wedding is to take place. When she is in bed, she is to drink a potion that he has made to induce sleep. The sleep will be so deep that no pulse can be found, and her body will be cold to the touch. The color will leave her face and she will appear as dead. She will stay in this condition 42 hours and then will awaken as from a pleasant sleep. When her family finds her early Thursday morning, they will take her to the family tomb where she will rest with Tybalt and those ancestors who have died. He, the Friar, will send letters to Romeo telling him of the plan, and he will be in the tomb waiting for her to awaken. Then, the two of them will go to Mantua.

Scene II finds Lord Capulet, the Nurse, and servants preparing for the wedding. Juliet returns from Friar Laurence's cell and goes directly to her father where she begs for his forgiveness. She says, "I beseech you! Henceforward I am ever ruled by you." Lord Capulet is so happy that she has returned to her original obedient nature that he sends for Paris to tell him that they can marry Wednesday instead of waiting for Thursday. Lord Capulet tells Lady Capulet to help Juliet, and he plans to stay up all night directing the servants in making preparations for the wedding that will take place in the morning, a day earlier than originally planned.

Scene III takes place within Juliet's chamber. She tells her mother that she needs no further help and that she needs to be left alone. As Juliet prepares to drink the potion, she becomes frightened and worries that if the potion does not work, she will have to marry Paris in the morning. To insure that this does not happen, she places her dagger beside her. A second worry is that possibly the potion is really poison, because the Friar might be afraid for his life since he was the one who married her to Romeo. A third worry is that she might awaken before Romeo gets there and because there is no air to breathe, she will suffocate. Her fourth worry is that she will awaken in the tomb, but the terror of the vault will be too much for her and she will lose her mind and kill herself.

Then she thinks she sees Tybalt's ghost coming for Romeo. It is this sight that enables her to summon up the courage to drink the potion.

Analysis

Act IV is considered the falling action of the play. The action moves swiftly and logically toward the tragedy that occurs at the end of the play. The consequences or forces that oppose the protagonists bring the ultimate end closer. The recent events have propelled the characters in one direction and the results are almost inevitable at this point. The tempo of the action increases from this act until the end of the play.

Juliet is experiencing internal conflict throughout this act and especially in Scenes I, II, and III. She has developed from a child into a woman who has fallen in love and married. She must act without Romeo and without the assistance of the nurse. She has disobeyed her parents by refusing to marry Paris, and lied about her reason for going to Friar Laurence's cell. She knows that she can not legally or morally marry Paris. Yet, she cannot tell her father about her marriage to Romeo. She also knows that by giving the impression of conformity and submitting to the wishes of her father, she can avoid any more confrontations and carry out the plan devised by the Friar. Her sense of betrayal by the nurse's advice to marry Paris has caused Juliet to feel that she has lost her closest friend and confidant. Juliet realizes that she must rely upon her own decisions and intuitions from now on. When she returns from Friar Laurence's cell and prepares to drink the potion, she is again struck with internal conflict. Her desperation is demonstrated by the fact that she places a dagger beside her in case the potion does not work. Rather than marry Paris, she will choose death.

Friar Laurence has become a pivotal character in the plot of the play. Some of his actions have been hasty and without proper reasoning. However, the Friar only wants good to come of his decisions. The reader was prepared for the use of the Friar's knowledge of herbs and plants from Act II, Scene III. This knowledge will be used in the potion Juliet is to drink. He has become a confidant to not only Romeo, but also Juliet. He is patient with the lovers as they threaten suicide in place of being apart. He has kept them from suicide and helped to find a solution to the dilemma that surrounds them. He is a neutral character who tries to end the violence in his society; however, his plans will cause the deaths of a number of characters.

Scene III contrasts drastically with the preceding one which was centered upon desperation, talk of death, conflict, and trouble. In this scene, there are happy preparations for a celebration of marriage. It is a domestic scene full of excitement and promises of new beginnings. It is dramatic irony that the audience or reader knows that because of the sleeping potion Juliet will not be a part of the joy, preparations, or celebration.

Juliet's final speech before she drinks the potion is a good example of the Shakespearean soliloquy. She deliberates its pros and cons before drinking the liquid. She is afraid that the potion will not work. She fears that Friar Laurence has given her poison to cover his part in the secret marriage to Romeo. She is afraid of awakening in the burial vault before Romeo arrives and not being able to breathe, and finally, she is afraid of going mad amid the horrors of the skeletons and smells that will surround her.

Study Questions

1. Why is Paris at Friar Laurence's cell?

2. What reason does Paris give the Friar for the hasty marriage?

3. How long will the sleeping potion take effect?

4. Where will Juliet be put after her family believes that she is dead?

5. Who will be waiting in the tomb when Juliet awakens from the sleeping potion?

6. Who is supervising the preparations for the wedding?

7. What change does Lord Capulet make in the wedding plans?

8. If the potion does not work, what does Juliet plan to do?

9. What vision makes her have the strength to go ahead and drink the potion?

10. How will Romeo know about the plans?

Answers

1. Paris is arranging his wedding with Friar Laurence.

2. The marriage is hasty in order to stop Juliet's tears over Tybalt's death.

3. The sleeping potion will last for 42 hours.

4. After her parents think she is dead, Juliet will be placed in the Capulet vault with her deceased ancestors.

5. When Juliet awakens from the sleeping potion, Romeo will be waiting for her in the tomb.

6. Lord Capulet is supervising the wedding preparations.

7. Lord Capulet moves the wedding from Thursday to Wednesday.

8. If the potion does not work, she plans to kill herself with the dagger that she lays beside her.

9. The vision of Tybalt coming after Romeo gives her the strength to go ahead and drink the potion.

10. Romeo will know of the plan because Friar Laurence is planning to send him a letter.

Suggested Essay Topics

1. Write a character sketch of Juliet emphasizing the internal conflict she is experiencing in this act.

2. How has the Friar's hobby contributed to the plot of the play?

3. Discuss the four fears Juliet experiences just before she drinks the sleeping potion.

Act IV, Scenes IV and V (pages 74–79)

Summary

Scene IV takes place in a hall of the Capulet's house. Lord and Lady Capulet, the Nurse, and numerous servants are busily preparing for the wedding. The Capulets and their servants are making jokes, not realizing that Juliet is in a deathlike trance in her room. She has risked her life in order to avoid what her family is celebrating. The curfew bell has just chimed three o'clock on Wednesday morning. Lord Capulet hears the music made by Paris and his company as they come for Juliet, and sends the Nurse to awaken and prepare her for the wedding.

Scene V is within Juliet's chamber. The Nurse comes into her room calling for her to get up because Paris is arriving. She calls her a "slugabed," a sleepy head, and draws back the curtains surrounding her bed. She believes that Juliet is dead and begins screaming. Lord and Lady Capulet rush into the room. Lord Capulet looks at her and exclaims, "She's cold, / Her blood is settled, and her joints are stiff; / Life and these lips have long been separated. / Death lies on her like an untimely frost." The Friar, Paris, and his musicians enter, and Lord Capulet tells them that Juliet is dead, and "Death is my son-in-law, Death is my heir; / My daughter he hath wedded." The love that the Capulets have for their daughter is indicated in the following lines: "Accursed, unhappy, wretched, hateful day!/ Most miserable hour that e'er time saw/ In lasting labour of his pilgrimage!/ But one, poor one, one poor and loving child,/ But one thing to rejoice and solace in,/ And cruel death hath catch'd it from my sight!" The anguish seems to be genuine even though earlier in the play Juliet's parents had wished that she "were married to her grave." The lines that Lord and Lady Capulet say are repetitive and exaggerated. Their grief does not raise sympathy in the audience or reader because of the knowledge that Juliet is not really dead.

The Friar, knowing that she is not really dead, attempts to comfort them by saying that they have done their part. Now, she belongs solely to Heaven. He consoles them and tells them to dry their eyes for she is better off in heaven. Lord Capulet decrees that everything that was to celebrate a wedding is to be changed befitting a funeral. The happiness of the wedding music will be changed to "melancholy bells." The hymns will change to dirges, and the bridal flowers will now become funeral flowers.

The scene ends with a comic discussion between the musicians and Peter.

Analysis

Compared to the volatile scene when Juliet refuses to marry Paris, Lord and Lady Capulet behave quite differently when they believe that she is dead. Lady Capulet's last words in Act III were "I would the fool were married to her grave!" Little did she realize that she was foreshadowing the future for her daughter. Lord Capulet, also, changed during the course of the play. In Act I, Lord Capulet tells Paris that "She is the hopeful lady of my earth." All his other children are dead and his life revolves around her; yet, he refuses to consider her feelings. Act III illustrates the anger and vengeance he threatens to take out on her if she does not marry Paris, and then, in Act IV, he swings full circle back to the doting and loving father. The Capulets' flaws center on their egos. They become too assured that they alone know what is best for their daughter. They do not have a close relationship with her and communicate poorly. In spite of these character flaws, they do love their only remaining child, and want what they believe to be the best for her.

It is interesting to watch the Friar lovingly and patiently console the parents because he knows all the circumstances. Some critics have wondered if the friar might be afraid of admitting his part in the uniting of the lovers because of the feud between the families.

There are many instances of dramatic irony in this act. Dramatic irony is a contrast between the audience's understanding of words and actions and the character's understanding. Juliet's meeting with Paris in Friar Laurence's cell is one example. Juliet is there to seek help in avoiding the very marriage that Paris is there trying to arrange. Another example are the wedding preparations by Lord Capulet. The Capulets and their servants are making jokes and busily preparing for the wedding, and the bride lies in her room in a deathlike trance. He is preparing for gaiety and happiness, and Juliet has taken a deathlike sleeping potion. The wedding arrangements will change into funeral arrangements. The ironic imagery of Juliet as the bride of death is illustrated in the lines, "The night before thy wedding-day/ Hath Death lain with thy wife. There she lies,/ Flower as she was, deflowered by him./ Death is my son-in-law, Death is my heir;/ My daughter he hath wedded." The emphasis on this tragic reversal anticipates the ending and is an example of tragedy as a reversal of expectations.

The final scene with Peter and the musicians provides the audience with comic relief. These men are not involved in Juliet's death and illustrate the fact that ordinary life goes on in spite of tragedy. Peter, who is himself a servant, enjoys making the musicians subservient to him.

Study Questions

1. Scene IV takes place at what time in the morning?

2. Scene IV takes place on what day?

3. How do the Capulets know that Paris is approaching?

4. Who is sent to wake up Juliet?

5. What does the Nurse find?

6. Who tries to console the Capulets by saying that Juliet is better off in heaven?

7. How do the wedding preparations change after they find Juliet?

8. How does the County Paris react to the death of Juliet?

9. How does Lord Capulet know that she is dead?

10. How does the act end?

Answers

1. Scene IV takes place at three in the morning.

2. Scene IV takes place early on Wednesday morning.

3. The Capulets know that Paris is coming because they can hear the music of his musicians.

4. The Nurse is sent to wake up Juliet.

5. The Nurse finds Juliet "dead" in her bed chamber.

6. The Friar tries to console the Capulets by assuring them that Juliet is in heaven.

7. The wedding preparations change dramatically. The wedding music becomes funeral dirges. The wedding flowers become funeral flowers, and the happiness associated with a wedding becomes sadness.

8. Paris is devastated by the news that Juliet is dead. He says, "Beguiled, divorced, wronged, spited, slain! / Most detestable Death, by thee beguiled, / By cruel, cruel thee quite overthrown. / O love! O life! not life, but love in death!"

9. Lord Capulet believes that Juliet is dead because he feels that her body is cold to the touch and her joints are stiff.

10. Act IV ends with a comic discussion between the musicians and Peter.

Suggested Essay Topics

1. Describe the reactions of Lord Capulet, Lady Capulet, the Nurse, and Friar Laurence to the death of Juliet.

2. Define dramatic irony and give examples from this act.

SECTION SIX

Act V

Act V, Scenes I and II (pages 80–84)

New Characters:

Balthasar: *a servant to Romeo*

Apothecary: *a druggist in Mantua who is extremely poor*

Friar John: *a Franciscan friar who is a friend to Friar Laurence*

Summary

Romeo is waiting for Balthasar to arrive with news from Verona. He is in Mantua and it is Thursday. He has had a dream that Juliet finds him dead, and she brings him back to life as an emperor with her kisses. Balthasar arrives telling Romeo that he saw Juliet buried in the Capulet tomb. Romeo says, "Then I defy you, stars!" and makes a hasty plan. He orders Balthasar to hire some fast horses and bring him ink and paper. Romeo inquires if there is a letter from the friar, and when the servant answers negatively, Romeo orders him to get what he demanded.

Romeo remembers an Apothecary in Mantua who appears to be extremely poor. Romeo decides to go to him and try to buy poison. It is against the law to sell poison in Mantua, but Romeo thinks he can sway the Apothecary to sell it to him because of his (the Apothecary's) extreme poverty.

Romeo offers the apothecary 40 ducats or gold pieces for the poison. At first, the man refuses to sell him the liquid, but reconsiders after Romeo reminds him of his extreme poverty. The Apothecary tells Romeo how to administer the poison, and

Romeo replies, "There is thy gold—worse poison to men's souls. / Doing more murder in this loathsome world, / Than these poor compounds that thou mayst not sell. / I sell thee poison; thou hast sold me none." After buying the poison, Romeo plans to go to Juliet's grave and die with her.

Scene 2 takes place in Friar Laurence's cell where he is welcoming Friar John from Mantua. Friar Laurence asks if there is a letter from Romeo, and Friar John tells him that he was not able to go to Mantua after all. While he was visiting the sick, the city authorities were afraid that the sickness might be the plague and quarantined the house. He was not allowed to leave the house or give the letter to a messenger to return to the Friar. Friar Laurence realizes that Romeo knows nothing of the plan to meet Juliet in the tomb and fears the worst. He asks Friar John to bring him a crow bar quickly, and he prepares to leave for the Capulet tomb where Juliet will be waking up within the next three hours.

Analysis

Events involving chance, circumstance, and coincidence in tragedy reinforce the notion of fate, and are considered beyond human control and contrary to men's best intentions. It is a coincidence that there happens to be a poor Apothecary who consents to sell Romeo the poison even if it is against the law. It is a matter of chance that the important letter relating the plans for Romeo and Juliet was not delivered by Friar John. The need for the delivery is coincident with the delay caused by the quarantine. Coincidence is also involved when Balthasar reports Juliet's death to Romeo before a true report is received from the friar. Romeo has no way of knowing that she is not dead. From this false knowledge, Romeo, being impetuous, acts too hastily and rushes to the Apothecary to purchase poison in order that he might die with Juliet. Through fate or the use of chance, circumstance, or coincidence, the resolution or conclusion of Act V is now inevitable.

Dreams and premonitions in the play, like foreshadowing, intensify the work of fate. Romeo has a dream of death in which he says,"My dreams presage some joyful news at hand;/ My bosom's lord sits lightly in his throne;/ And all this day an unaccustom'd spirit/ Lifts me above the ground with cheerful thoughts./ I dreamt my lady came and found me dead/ Strange dream, that gives a dead man leave to think/ And breathed such life with kisses in my lips,/ That I revived, and was an emperor." His dream of death is soon to be fulfilled and Juliet will kiss him on the lips. She will not awaken him, but she will join him in death.

The sickness that was so feared by the authorities that it caused them to quarantine Friar John was the bubonic plague. This plague killed millions of people in Europe, and its causes were not understood by the people. It is ironic that the authorities, through a fear of death by the plague, kept Friar John from delivering the letter, because the undelivered letter caused many deaths not related to the plague.

Romeo always considered suicide the final solution if he cannot live with Juliet. Thus, it is no surprise that, upon learning of Juliet's "death," he immediately goes to purchase poison. After Romeo buys the poison he says, "Come, cordial and not poison, go with me/ To Juliet's grave; for there must I use thee." Romeo's verbal irony is that the poison, because it will reunite him with Juliet, is really a restorative medicine. It was believed that a "cordial" was a kind of medicine that restored the heartbeat.

Study Questions

1. Where does Scene I take place?

2. What was Romeo's dream?

3. Who brings Romeo the news that Juliet is dead?

4. Why does Romeo go to the Apothecary?

5. How much does Romeo pay for the poison?

6. Why does the Apothecary hesitate in selling Romeo the poison?

7. What persuades the Apothecary to go ahead and sell Romeo the poison?

8. Who does Friar Laurence entrust with the important letter to Romeo?

9. Why is the letter not delivered to Romeo?

10. How long will it be before Juliet wakes up?

Answers

1. Scene I takes place in Mantua where Romeo has been banished.

2. Romeo dreams that Juliet finds him dead and brings him back to life as an emperor with her kisses.

3. Balthasar, Romeo's servant, brings him the news that Juliet is dead and was buried in the Capulet tomb.

4. Romeo goes to the Apothecary to buy poison.

5. Romeo pays 40 ducats for the poison.

6. The Apothecary hesitates in selling Romeo the poison because it is against the law in Mantua to sell the substance.

7. Because of his extreme poverty, the Apothecary consents to sell Romeo the poison.

8. Friar Laurence entrusts the important letter to Friar John to deliver to Romeo. This letter explains to Romeo about Juliet's pretended death and tells him to be at the tomb when she wakes up.

9. Friar John is not able to deliver the letter because he is quarantined while visiting the sick.

10. Juliet is due to wake up in about three hours.

Suggested Essay Topics

1. What coincidences occur in this act?

2. Explain fully what goes wrong with Friar Laurence's plan to reunite the lovers.

Act V, Scene III (pages 84–92)

New Characters:

Page: *a servant to Paris*

Summary

Scene III takes place in the churchyard where the Capulet monument is located. Paris and the Page are outside the tomb of Juliet. Paris instructs the page to put out the torch and stand guard while he enters the tomb. The Page is to whistle if anyone approaches. As Paris begins to enter the tomb the Page whistles, indicating that someone is near. Paris watches as Romeo and Balthasar approach. Romeo instructs Balthasar to give a letter to his father the next morning and not to intervene with his purpose. Romeo tells Balthasar that the reason he is at the tomb is to look upon Juliet's face and to remove a ring from her finger. Balthasar is then instructed to leave the churchyard under the penalty of death by Romeo if he fails to obey him.

Balthasar does not believe Romeo's reasons for being at the tomb and fears for his master. Because of his concern for Romeo, Balthasar hides nearby rather than leave the churchyard.

As Romeo enters the tomb, Paris recognizes him as Romeo, the one who killed Tybalt and caused Juliet so much grief. Paris believes that he has come to the tomb to do some "vile outrage" to the bodies of Tybalt and Juliet. He steps forward and tries to prevent Romeo from entering the tomb. Because Paris has no torch, Romeo does not recognize him. They fight, and Paris is killed. As they fight, the Page runs for help. After Paris falls fatally wounded, Romeo looks upon his face and realizes that it is Paris. He remembers Balthasar telling him something about Juliet being promised to marry Paris, so he decides to bury him also in the tomb with Juliet. Romeo drags Paris' body into the Capulet tomb and goes to Juliet's side.

As he embraces Juliet, Romeo talks about her beauty even in death. Her lips and cheeks are crimson, and he notices that even Death cannot take away her beauty. He embraces her, kisses her one last time, and joins her in death by drinking the poison.

At this point, Friar Laurence enters the churchyard and stumbles upon Balthasar who is hiding. Balthasar tells the friar that Romeo has been in the tomb about half an hour and he is afraid. The Friar is afraid that something has happened and rushes into the tomb. He finds the bodies of Paris and Romeo. Juliet is just beginning to stir, and upon recognizing the friar, she asks about Romeo. The Friar hears the night guard coming and knowing that he could be implicated in the murder, becomes frightened and begs Juliet to accompany him outside. He tells her that their plans have gone awry and Paris, as well as Romeo, are dead. He promises to take her to a place where nuns live. Juliet refuses to leave and the friar, rather than be discovered, does not even stay to help Juliet, but flees.

Juliet notices the cup in Romeo's hand and knows that it is poison that has ended her lover's life. She tries to drink just one drop to kill herself, but she finds nothing left in the cup. She kisses him and realizes that his lips are still warm. Upon hearing the watchmen approaching, she takes Romeo's dagger and kills herself.

The watchmen enter the tomb and find the bodies of Paris, Romeo, and Juliet, who supposedly died two days ago. Yet, her body is warm and newly dead. The Capulets and the Montagues are sent for as the watchmen begin to bring in suspects. One watchman brings Balthasar into the tomb, and another watchman finds Friar Laurence. The Prince arrives and inquires about the deaths. When the Capulets arrive, Lord Capulet notices that Romeo's dagger is the one that was used to kill his daughter and assumes that Romeo is responsible for her death. Lord Montague enters and tells the Prince that grief over Romeo's exile has also caused Lady Montague's death.

The Prince demands that the cries of vengeance be stopped until the truth can be discovered. He orders that the "parties of suspicion" be brought forward. The Friar admits to being the most suspected because he was caught leaving the churchyard carrying instruments to break into a tomb. Finally the Friar is forced to relate the entire story concerning Romeo and Juliet. He tells how they were married and her father demanded that she marry Paris. He tells of the plan for Juliet to drink the sleeping potion, be reunited with Romeo after 42 hours, and the accidental quarantine that prevented his letter from reaching Romeo. The Friar accepts the responsibility for what has happened and says, "Let my old life be sacrificed some hour before his time / Unto the rigor of severest law." The Prince says that Friar Laurence is a holy man and turns to question Balthasar.

Balthasar tells the Prince how he brought news of Juliet's death to Romeo in Mantua. He relates how they arrived at the tomb and Romeo gave him the letter that was to have gone to Lord Montague the next morning.

The Page is then instructed to tell his side of the story. He relates how his master came to Juliet's grave to bring flowers and weep. Paris was startled when Romeo approached the tomb, and fearing that Romeo wanted to do some damage to the bodies, tried to arrest him. Paris and Romeo fought and Paris was killed.

After reading the letter, the Prince declares that all the Friar had said was true. Because of the hatred between the Capulets and Montagues, both sides have lost many loved ones. The Capulets and Montagues shake hands and decide to build gold statues in honor of their children. Their children were "poor sacrifices of our enmity." The play ends with the Prince saying that there was never a story sadder than the one of Romeo and Juliet.

Analysis

The conclusion or catastrophe takes place in Scene III of the play. The conclusion quickly draws to a close as almost all the characters are on stage for various reasons. This last scene reveals one death not witnessed and three that are performed on stage. The predictions issued at the beginning of the play by the Chorus have all been fulfilled. Each scene contributes to the plot and focuses on the lovers' plight. This scene contains more examples of fate or coincidence and how it controlled the lives of the lovers.

Some illustrations of the workings of fate through chance or coincidence are Romeo's suicide just before Juliet awakens, Friar Laurence arriving just a little too late to save him, and even Juliet's death. If Romeo had not been so hasty, he would have realized that Juliet was not dead. Just a small hesitation on his part would have allowed her to awaken. Again, Romeo and Juliet's hastiness play a part in their destruction. The deaths are not only a testimony to the force of fate working through chance, coincidence, change or reversal, circumstance, and personal flaws, but to the power of their love.

Again, light transforms the darkness when he first sees Juliet in the tomb and says, "For here lies Juliet, and her beauty makes/ This vault a feasting presence full of light." The love that they saw in one another's presence was a source of warmth and light. The theme of light and dark is present even in the last scene of the play.

Irony also plays a part as the families honor the lovers in death although they would have refused to recognize their love while they were alive. Romeo and Juliet lived in a culture that was unsympathetic toward love and idealism. The violence and hatred present in their society naturally bred tragedy.

Romeo's speech as he opens the Capulet tomb contains many examples of metaphorical language. He says, "Thou detestable maw, thou womb of death, / Gorged with the dearest morsel of the earth, / Thus I enforce thy rotten jaws to open, / And in despite I'll cram thee with more food." Romeo is comparing the tomb to a detestable maw, and a womb of death. The dearest morsel of the earth is referring to Juliet and the jaws refer to the mouth of the tomb itself. His death fulfills the reference of cramming the tomb with more food. Death is personified as her love—an image foreshadowed earlier.

In the final scene, the Prince says, "See what a scourge is laid upon your hate, / That heaven finds means to kill your joys with love." It is ironic that love could kill joy, but the love shared by Romeo and Juliet ultimately ended their lives. Romeo and Juliet were the "joys" of the Montague and Capulet families. It was because of the hate between the families that the children were afraid to make their love known.

One of the causes of this tragedy is that the flaw of impulsiveness is shared by many of the characters. Friar Laurence, Tybalt, Lord Capulet, Romeo, Mercutio, Juliet, and even the Nurse all contribute to the tragedy through impulsiveness, which is the real villain in the play. Shakespeare illustrated the rashness in the old and young alike in a universal way. Chance or fate plays a role in this tragedy, but the importance of character and the actions stemming from it are equally important. The connection of character with his deed and then to the tragedy sets the course for the catastrophe, and its outcome is inevitable.

The universality of Shakespeare's plays make the reader or audience realize that time does not alter human nature, and Romeo and Juliet have become symbols of youthful romance. Hate breeds violence and death, and love can transcend all earthly rules and boundaries.

Study Questions

1. Why is Paris at Juliet's tomb?

2. What is Paris' last request?

3. Why does Paris think Romeo has come to the Capulet tomb?

4. Who kills Paris?

5. If Romeo had not been so hasty in drinking the poison, what would he have noticed about Juliet?

6. Name the people who have died in this scene.

7. Where does Friar Laurence want to take Juliet?

8. How does Juliet kill herself?

9. Who is suspected the most as a murderer and why?

10. What four accounts does the Prince hear?

Answers

1. Paris has come to Juliet's tomb to bring flowers and weep.

2. As he dies, Paris' last request is to lie beside Juliet.

3. Paris believes that Romeo has come to the tomb to do damage to the bodies of Tybalt and Juliet.

4. Romeo kills Paris.

5. If Romeo had not been so hasty in drinking the poison, he would have understood why Juliet's lips and cheeks were crimson. She was beginning to wake up from the potion.

6. Paris, Lady Montague, Romeo, and Juliet have all died in this scene.

7. When Juliet wakes up, Friar Laurence is there and wants to take her to a "sisterhood of holy nuns."

8. Juliet kills herself with Romeo's dagger.

9. Friar Laurence is suspected the most because he is carrying tools for digging and opening tombs.

10. When the Prince wants to know what has happened, Friar Laurence, Balthasar, the Page, and the contents of the letter in Balthasar's possession all give the same account of the events.

Suggested Essay Topics

1. Describe the role of Friar Laurence in the play and how he contributes to the fate of the lovers.

2. Explain in detail how Romeo and Juliet both mature during the course of the play. Cite examples from their speech or actions that illustrate your position.

3. How have the deaths of Romeo and Juliet affected the entire city of Verona?

4. Discuss the role of chance or coincidence in the play. How did it affect the ending of the play?

5. Discuss the role of Paris in the play.

Bibliography

Craig, Hardin, Ed. *The Complete Works of Shakespeare*. Chicago: Scott, Foresman and Company, 1961.

Kittredge, George Lyman, Ed. *The Kittredge-Players Edition of the Complete Works of William Shakespeare*. New York: Grolier, 1936.

Prentice Hall Literature: Gold. New Jersey: Prentice Hall, Inc., 1989.

Toor, David. *A Life of Shakespeare. New York: Kenilworth Press,* 1976.

FICTION

FLATLAND: A ROMANCE OF MANY DIMENSIONS, Edwin A. Abbott. (0-486-27263-X)

PRIDE AND PREJUDICE, Jane Austen. (0-486-28473-5)

CIVIL WAR SHORT STORIES AND POEMS, Edited by Bob Blaisdell. (0-486-48226-X)

THE DECAMERON: Selected Tales, Giovanni Boccaccio. Edited by Bob Blaisdell. (0-486-41113-3)

JANE EYRE, Charlotte Brontë. (0-486-42449-9)

WUTHERING HEIGHTS, Emily Brontë. (0-486-29256-8)

THE THIRTY-NINE STEPS, John Buchan. (0-486-28201-5)

ALICE'S ADVENTURES IN WONDERLAND, Lewis Carroll. (0-486-27543-4)

MY ÁNTONIA, Willa Cather. (0-486-28240-6)

THE AWAKENING, Kate Chopin. (0-486-27786-0)

HEART OF DARKNESS, Joseph Conrad. (0-486-26464-5)

LORD JIM, Joseph Conrad. (0-486-40650-4)

THE RED BADGE OF COURAGE, Stephen Crane. (0-486-26465-3)

THE WORLD'S GREATEST SHORT STORIES, Edited by James Daley. (0-486-44716-2)

A CHRISTMAS CAROL, Charles Dickens. (0-486-26865-9)

GREAT EXPECTATIONS, Charles Dickens. (0-486-41586-4)

A TALE OF TWO CITIES, Charles Dickens. (0-486-40651-2)

CRIME AND PUNISHMENT, Fyodor Dostoyevsky. Translated by Constance Garnett. (0-486-41587-2)

THE ADVENTURES OF SHERLOCK HOLMES, Sir Arthur Conan Doyle. (0-486-47491-7)

THE HOUND OF THE BASKERVILLES, Sir Arthur Conan Doyle. (0-486-28214-7)

BLAKE: PROPHET AGAINST EMPIRE, David V. Erdman. (0-486-26719-9)

WHERE ANGELS FEAR TO TREAD, E. M. Forster. (0-486-27791-7)

BEOWULF, Translated by R. K. Gordon. (0-486-27264-8)

THE RETURN OF THE NATIVE, Thomas Hardy. (0-486-43165-7)

THE SCARLET LETTER, Nathaniel Hawthorne. (0-486-28048-9)

SIDDHARTHA, Hermann Hesse. (0-486-40653-9)

THE ODYSSEY, Homer. (0-486-40654-7)

THE TURN OF THE SCREW, Henry James. (0-486-26684-2)

DUBLINERS, James Joyce. (0-486-26870-5)

NONFICTION

POETICS, Aristotle. (0-486-29577-X)

MEDITATIONS, Marcus Aurelius. (0-486-29823-X)

THE WAY OF PERFECTION, St. Teresa of Avila. Edited and Translated by E. Allison Peers. (0-486-48451-3)

THE DEVIL'S DICTIONARY, Ambrose Bierce. (0-486-27542-6)

GREAT SPEECHES OF THE 20TH CENTURY, Edited by Bob Blaisdell. (0-486-47467-4)

THE COMMUNIST MANIFESTO AND OTHER REVOLUTIONARY WRITINGS: Marx, Marat, Paine, Mao Tse-Tung, Gandhi and Others, Edited by Bob Blaisdell. (0-486-42465-0)

INFAMOUS SPEECHES: From Robespierre to Osama bin Laden, Edited by Bob Blaisdell. (0-486-47849-1)

GREAT ENGLISH ESSAYS: From Bacon to Chesterton, Edited by Bob Blaisdell. (0-486-44082-6)

GREEK AND ROMAN ORATORY, Edited by Bob Blaisdell. (0-486-49622-8)

THE UNITED STATES CONSTITUTION: The Full Text with Supplementary Materials, Edited and with supplementary materials by Bob Blaisdell. (0-486-47166-7)

GREAT SPEECHES BY NATIVE AMERICANS, Edited by Bob Blaisdell. (0-486-41122-2)

GREAT SPEECHES BY AFRICAN AMERICANS: Frederick Douglass, Sojourner Truth, Dr. Martin Luther King, Jr., Barack Obama, and Others, Edited by James Daley. (0-486-44761-8)

GREAT SPEECHES BY AMERICAN WOMEN, Edited by James Daley. (0-486-46141-6)

HISTORY'S GREATEST SPEECHES, Edited by James Daley. (0-486-49739-9)

GREAT INAUGURAL ADDRESSES, Edited by James Daley. (0-486-44577-1)

GREAT SPEECHES ON GAY RIGHTS, Edited by James Daley. (0-486-47512-3)

ON THE ORIGIN OF SPECIES: By Means of Natural Selection, Charles Darwin. (0-486-45006-6)

NARRATIVE OF THE LIFE OF FREDERICK DOUGLASS, Frederick Douglass. (0-486-28499-9)

THE SOULS OF BLACK FOLK, W. E. B. Du Bois. (0-486-28041-1)

NATURE AND OTHER ESSAYS, Ralph Waldo Emerson. (0-486-46947-6)

SELF-RELIANCE AND OTHER ESSAYS, Ralph Waldo Emerson. (0-486-27790-9)

THE LIFE OF OLAUDAH EQUIANO, Olaudah Equiano. (0-486-40661-X)

WIT AND WISDOM FROM POOR RICHARD'S ALMANACK, Benjamin Franklin. (0-486-40891-4)

THE AUTOBIOGRAPHY OF BENJAMIN FRANKLIN, Benjamin Franklin. (0-486-29073-5)

PLAYS

THE ORESTEIA TRILOGY: Agamemnon, the Libation-Bearers and the Furies, Aeschylus. (0-486-29242-8)

EVERYMAN, Anonymous. (0-486-28726-2)

THE BIRDS, Aristophanes. (0-486-40886-8)

LYSISTRATA, Aristophanes. (0-486-28225-2)

THE CHERRY ORCHARD, Anton Chekhov. (0-486-26682-6)

THE SEA GULL, Anton Chekhov. (0-486-40656-3)

MEDEA, Euripides. (0-486-27548-5)

FAUST, PART ONE, Johann Wolfgang von Goethe. (0-486-28046-2)

THE INSPECTOR GENERAL, Nikolai Gogol. (0-486-28500-6)

SHE STOOPS TO CONQUER, Oliver Goldsmith. (0-486-26867-5)

GHOSTS, Henrik Ibsen. (0-486-29852-3)

A DOLL'S HOUSE, Henrik Ibsen. (0-486-27062-9)

HEDDA GABLER, Henrik Ibsen. (0-486-26469-6)

DR. FAUSTUS, Christopher Marlowe. (0-486-28208-2)

TARTUFFE, Molière. (0-486-41117-6)

BEYOND THE HORIZON, Eugene O'Neill. (0-486-29085-9)

THE EMPEROR JONES, Eugene O'Neill. (0-486-29268-1)

CYRANO DE BERGERAC, Edmond Rostand. (0-486-41119-2)

MEASURE FOR MEASURE: Unabridged, William Shakespeare. (0-486-40889-2)

FOUR GREAT TRAGEDIES: Hamlet, Macbeth, Othello, and Romeo and Juliet, William Shakespeare. (0-486-44083-4)

THE COMEDY OF ERRORS, William Shakespeare. (0-486-42461-8)

HENRY V, William Shakespeare. (0-486-42887-7)

MUCH ADO ABOUT NOTHING, William Shakespeare. (0-486-28272-4)

FIVE GREAT COMEDIES: Much Ado About Nothing, Twelfth Night, A Midsummer Night's Dream, As You Like It and The Merry Wives of Windsor, William Shakespeare. (0-486-44086-9)

OTHELLO, William Shakespeare. (0-486-29097-2)

AS YOU LIKE IT, William Shakespeare. (0-486-40432-3)

ROMEO AND JULIET, William Shakespeare. (0-486-27557-4)

A MIDSUMMER NIGHT'S DREAM, William Shakespeare. (0-486-27067-X)

THE MERCHANT OF VENICE, William Shakespeare. (0-486-28492-1)

HAMLET, William Shakespeare. (0-486-27278-8)

RICHARD III, William Shakespeare. (0-486-28747-5)